Green Wheat

Green Wheat

A NOVEL
Colette

TRANSLATED BY
Zack Rogow

Sarabande Books
LOUISVILLE, KENTUCKY

Managing Editor
Sarabande Books, Inc.
2234 Dundee Road, Suite 200
Louisville, KY 40205

Library of Congress Cataloging-in-Publication Data
Colette, 1873–1954.
    [Blé en herbe. English]
    Green wheat : a novella / by Colette ; [translated by Zack Rogow].—1st ed.
        p.   cm.
    ISBN 1-932511-01-6 (pbk. : alk. paper)
I. Rogow, Zack. II. Title.
PQ2605.O28 B513 2004
843'.912—dc21   2003013540

Cover and text design by Charles Casey Martin

Printed in Canada
This book is printed on acid-free paper.

Sarabande Books is a nonprofit literary organization.

 This project is supported in part by an award from the
NATIONAL
ENDOWMENT National Endowment for the Arts.
FOR THE ARTS

FIRST EDITION

• ACKNOWLEDGMENTS •

The translator wishes to thank Renée Morel and William Rodarmor for reading this English version and for making many helpful suggestions that were incorporated into the text.

• TRANSLATOR'S PREFACE •

OF HER MORE THAN TWENTY BOOKS, *Green Wheat* is perhaps Colette's most polished, most perfect. It was in *Green Wheat* that she achieved an exquisite blend of two of her greatest gifts as a fiction writer— her uncanny ability to fathom the hearts of adolescents, and her skill at describing nature with the phrasing of a poet and the colors and light of a great landscape painter. This combination helps make *Green Wheat* one of the enduring works of fiction of the last 100 years.

The French newspaper *Le Matin* originally serialized *Green Wheat* beginning in July 1922. Even though Colette's husband, the Baron Henry de Jouvenel, was the paper's editor, the uproar among the readers at the book's frank depiction of adolescent sexuality forced *Le Matin* to cease publication before the final chapters were printed. In *Green Wheat* Colette has a keen eye for the way that sex figures into the thoughts and emotions of her protagonists, the fifteen- and sixteen-year-old Vinca and Phil. Her intent is not primarily sensationalistic, but an attempt to be true to life. She's also ahead of her time and amazingly realistic in showing the extremes of adolescence from within, conveying the feelings behind suicidal urges and teenagers' masklike opacity toward adults.

The book is also realistic in its use of slangy dialogue between its two main characters. It even begins with a broken sentence that announces from the start that the reader will see and hear real teenagers, not a syrupy version of their world: "You going fishing, Vinca?"

The vividness of the dialogue and the need to provide an uncensored account of the action are reasons a new translation seems in order. I'm not trying to turn Vinca into a Valley Girl. My intent is to render the spoken lines in an English that tries to do justice to Colette's enormous talent for portraying the actual speech of young people, and to honor her foresight and brilliance in giving an accurate picture of teenage life.

Explaining the genesis of her novel to an interviewer, Colette said, "...for a long, long time I'd wanted to write a piece for the Théâtre-Français.... The curtain rises, the stage is plunged in darkness, two invisible characters expound on their love with wisdom and experience. Toward the last lines, the lights come up and the surprised audience sees that the couple are fifteen and sixteen years old. I wanted to show that passionate love has no age and that love does not have two separate languages.... I wasn't saying anything else in *Green Wheat*. I just interspersed with the narrative a few landscapes from the region of Cancale that moved me."

These landscapes from Brittany that Colette weaves into the novel are another extraordinary feature of the book. They're not just interspersed, they're sketched with incredible sensitivity, and they unobtrusively mirror the emotions of the characters. The natural descriptions also provide a seasonal clock of the span of the novel, one summer vacation, and that clock ticks toward the novel's inevitable end. "August was going down in flames," writes Colette when Phil encounters the villa of the older woman in the novel's love triangle. Describing a rainy day when Phil and Vinca feel trapped in a waiting game before they can have a real life together, Colette includes this passage, "He wiped the sand off his hands on a clump of moist wild thyme, laden with flowers and little hornets trapped by the rain, who waited numbly for the next ray of sun." These descriptions are not just poetry. They take the reader farther into the heightened world of adolescents, where small moments often resonate deeply. In fact all the description in the book, both interior and exterior, has the magnified awareness of teenagers, piercing and fabulous at the same time.

But Colette's *Green Wheat* isn't merely an exercise in painting the world of young people. The book is in some ways a *roman à clef*, an attempt by the author to make sense of her own role in a romantic snarl of knots that involved Colette, her husband Henry de Jouvenel, Henry's lovers, Henry's son and Colette's stepson Bertrand de Jouvenel, and a fifteen-year-old English girl named Pamela whom Bertrand was in love with when he was sixteen.

Henry de Jouvenel neglected his wife, Colette, and his son for his political career and his other lovers. He was both a well-known, left-leaning newspaper editor and an important politician, elected to serve in the Senate and appointed by the French president as France's chief delegate to the League of Nations.

Partly in revenge for Henry's leaving her bed for another, Colette seduced her virgin stepson, Bertrand, while they were vacationing at her country house in Brittany in the summer of 1920, at the same time that Bertrand was infatuated with the young Pamela. "It is tempting but too facile to see Colette as a sexual predator and to underestimate Bertrand's active, even aggressive (or at least passively aggressive) complicity in the affair," writes Judith Thurman in her recent biography, *The Secrets of the Flesh: A Life of Colette*. In fact the affair was no mere caprice, but continued off and on for almost five years, even after the book publication of *Green Wheat* in 1923.

Colette herself provided a trail to connect *Green Wheat* to her liaison with Bertrand. She named the older woman in her novel Madame Dalleray, and when Bertrand was in Paris he often stayed at the apartment of their friend Hélène Picard on the rue d'Alleray.

I mention this connection to Colette's life not to gossip (well, maybe partly to gossip!), but mainly to point out the enormous complexity of the emotions in the novel. *Green Wheat* explores guilt, but also rapture and loyalty. Ultimately the book is a story about the loss of an Eden, both of youth and of nature. In Colette's surprisingly contemporary version of the biblical tale, innocence is not what's at stake—innocence has little to do with adolescence in Colette's view. *Green Wheat* is actually about the loss of a type of hope, a hope that many of us cling to, that love can somehow escape the imperfections of life.

Zack Rogow
San Francisco, February 2002

Green Wheat

"You going fishing, Vinca?"

With a haughty toss of her head, Vinca—"Periwinkle"—her eyes the color of spring rain, answered that yes, she was going fishing. Her mended sweater testified to it, and so did her espadrilles, stiffened by salt. It was clear that her blue and green checked skirt, already three years old and short enough to show her knees, belonged to the shrimp and crabs. And those two nets she carried over her shoulder, and that woolen beret, shaggy and bluish as a thistle on the dunes, didn't they make up a fishing gear of sorts?

Vinca passed the boy who had waved to her. She walked down toward the rocks, taking long strides with her thin and well-turned spindles, the color of terra cotta. Philippe watched her walking, placing Vinca side by side with the Vinca of the previous summer. Was she fully grown? It was high time for her to stop. Her body was no fleshier than last year. Her short hair scattered into stiff, gilded straw that she had been growing out for four months, but she still could not braid or curl it. Her cheeks and hands were blackened by the sun, her neck white as milk under her hair, her smile forced, her laugh explosive, and though she buttoned her jackets and sweaters tightly over an imaginary bust, she hiked up her skirts and trousers as high as she could to walk down to the water, with the calmness of a young boy.

Her friend, who was spying on her, lay on the dunes with their long, furry grasses, and cradled in his crossed arms his chin split by a dimple. He was sixteen and a half, now that Vinca had reached fifteen and a half. Their entire childhoods bound them together, adolescence pulled them apart. The year before they had already exchanged bitter words, a few surreptitious punches; now silence could suddenly fall between them so heavily that they preferred sulking to the effort of conversation. But Philippe was cunning. He was born to hunt and play tricks, and he veiled his silence in mystery, bending everything that embarrassed him into a weapon. He tried on worldly gestures, risked a "What's the use?... You wouldn't understand...." while Vinca could only keep quiet, suffering from what she was keeping in, from what she wanted to learn, and she steeled herself against the precocious and imperious instinct to give everything, against the fear that Philippe, who changed a little bit more every day, and every hour grew stronger, would break the frail string that pulled him back, each year, from July to October, to the tufted woods sloping down to the sea, to the rocks with their shaggy heads of black seaweed. He already had a deadly way of staring at his friend, not seeing her, as if Vinca were transparent, liquid, insignificant.

Probably next year she would fall at his feet and say to him in a womanly voice, "Phil! Don't be cruel...I love you, Phil, do what you want with me.... Speak to me, Phil...." But this year she still kept the rough dignity of childhood, she resisted, and Phil resented that resistance.

He looked over the girl, flat and graceful, who was just then walking down to the sea. He no more desired to kiss her than to hit her, but he did want her to trust him, to be his alone, to be available like those treasures that now made him blush—dried petals, agate marbles, shells and seeds, pictures, a little silver watch....

"Wait up, Vinca! I'm coming fishing!" he yelled.

She slowed her pace without turning back. He caught up with her in a few leaps and grabbed one of her nets.

"Why did you bring two?"

"I took the little pouch for the nooks and crannies, and my own net, like I always do."

His softest, black glance dove into her blue eyes:

5

"So, you didn't bring it for *me?*"

At the same time he held out his hand to help her jump over the worst corridor in the rocks, and the blood rose into Vinca's sunburnt cheeks. Any new gesture or look was enough to confound her. Yesterday they roamed the cliffs, explored the depths of the pools side by side—each at his own risk. She was as nimble as he was—she didn't remember ever needing Phil's help.

"How about a little sweetness, Vinca!" he pleaded, smiling, since she had jaggedly pulled her hand back. "What've you got against me?"

She bit her lip, cracked by her daily diving, and stepped over the rocks bristling with acorn barnacles. She examined her own thoughts and saw mistrust. What was up with *him?* Suddenly he was obliging, charming, and offered her his hand as if to a lady. She slowly lowered the little pouch of thread into a cavity where the sea water, motionless, revealed algae, sea-slugs, catfish, scorpion fish all heads and fins, black crabs with red braid, and shrimp. Phil's shadow obscured the sunlit pool.

"Move over! Your shadow is blocking the shrimp, and this is my fishing hole!"

He didn't persist and she fished by herself, impatient, not her usual adept self. Ten, twenty shrimp escaped the rough swoops of her net and cowered in the fissures where their delicate beards tested the water and defied the trap.

"Phil, c'mere, Phil! The place is swarming with shrimp, and they won't let me catch them!"

He walked over casually and leaned over the little, teaming abyss:

"Well, what do you expect? You don't know what you're doing."

"I do, too!" Vinca protested bitterly. "I just don't have the patience."

Phil plunged his net into the water and held it still.

"In the cranny of that rock," Vinca whispered from behind his shoulder, "there are some real beauties. Can't you see their horns?"

"No. Doesn't matter. They'll come in good time."

"You really think so?"

"Sure. Look."

She leaned over farther, and her hair—like a short, trapped wing—swiped her friend's cheek. She recoiled, then moved imperceptibly closer again, only to recoil once more. He acted as if he didn't notice, but his free hand pulled Vinca's naked, sunburnt and salty arm.

"Look, Vinca. There's a real beaut."

Vinca's arm, which she was now slipping away, slid down to Phil's wrist, then into his hand as if into a bracelet, since he didn't squeeze it.

"You won't get her, Phil, she's gone."

To follow the play of the shrimp better, Vinca slid her arm up to the elbow back into his half-closed hand. In the green water, the tall, gray agate shrimp was testing the edge of the net with the tip of its hooks, with the tip of its beard. One flick of the wrist and.... But the fisherman waited too long, perhaps savoring the motionless arm, docile to his touch, the weight of a head veiled in hair leaning against his shoulder, momentarily defeated, then swerving away, wildly....

"Quick, Phil, quick, pull up the net!... Oh, she's gone! Why did you let her get away?"

Phil took a deep breath and shot his friend a look where his pride, astonished, momentarily scorned its victory; he gave her back her thin arm, which didn't crave its freedom at all, and as he stirred the whole bright pool with a stroke of his net, he said, "Oh, she'll come back. It's just a matter of time...."

They swam side by side, his skin whiter, his head black and round under his wet hair, while she was burnt like a blonde, with a blue scarf tied around her hair. The daily swim was a complete and silent joy, and it allowed their awkward age a measure of peace and childhood, both precarious. Vinca lay down on the sea, spouting water into the air like a baby seal. The twisted scarf revealed not only her delicate, pink ears sheltered from the sun by her hair, but also those clearings of white skin at her temples that saw the light of day only when she swam. She smiled at Philippe, and under the eleven o'clock sun the delicious blue of her irises turned a bit green, reflecting the sea. Her friend suddenly dove down, grabbed one of Vinca's feet, and pulled her under a wave. They "drank" together, reappeared spitting, puffing, and laughing as if she had forgotten her fifteen years tormented by love for her childhood companion; and he had lost the memory of his sixteen years of domination, his pretty-boy's disdain, and his demands as a precocious proprietor.

"First one to the rock!" he yelled, splitting the water.

But Vinca didn't follow him, and strode up onto the nearby sand.

"You already leaving?"

She pulled off her scarf as if scalping herself, and shook out her stiff blonde hair:

"There's a man coming for lunch. Papa said we had to dress up."

She ran, so wet, tall, and boyish, but slender, with each long muscle standing out. A word from Philippe stopped her in her tracks.

"You're dressing up? What about me? Can't I have lunch with my shirt unbuttoned?"

"Sure, Phil! Anything you want. Anyway, you look a lot better with your shirt open!"

With her little mask wet and sunburnt, the eyes of the Periwinkle suddenly expressed anguish, pleading, a rough desire for approval. He maintained a haughty silence and Vinca clambered up the meadow by the sea blooming with sweet scabious.

Phil grumbled to himself, slapping the water. He hardly thought about what Vinca wanted. "I've always been handsome enough for her.... This year she never seems satisfied, though!"

And the apparent contradiction in these two notions made him smile. He took his turn at rolling onto his back on the waves, letting the salt water fill his ears with a rumbling silence. As a small cloud covered the high sun, Phil opened his eyes and saw passing overhead shadowed bellies; huge, tapered beaks; and the dark claws, bent back in flight, of a couple of curlews.

"Ridiculous idea," Phil said to himself. "No, really, what got into her? She looks like a dressed-up monkey. She looks like a mulatto about to take Communion...."

Next to Vinca, a little sister, more or less a copy of her, opened her blue eyes in a round, toasted face, under a dense thatch of blonde hair, and pressed down onto the tablecloth, next to her plate, the neatly folded hands of a well-behaved child. The older and younger daughters had on matching white dresses, ironed, starched, in organdy with flounces.

"Sunday in Tahiti," scoffed Phil to himself. "I've never seen her look so ugly."

Vinca's mother, Vinca's father, Vinca's aunt, Phil and his parents, the visiting Parisian ringed the table with green pullovers, striped blazers, tussore jackets. The families, who were friends, rented the villa every year. This morning it smelled of warm brioche and floor wax. The man going gray, who had come from Paris, was cast for the role, among these motley swimmers and blackened children, of the stranger—delicate, pale, and well-dressed.

"Vinca honey, just look at you, the way you're changing!" he said to the girl.

"You can say that again," muttered Phil peevishly.

The stranger leaned over toward Vinca's mother and confessed in half-whisper:

"She's becoming a stunner! Stunning. In two years... wait till you see her!"

Vinca overheard this, flashed the stranger a lively feminine glance, and smiled. Her crimson mouth split over a blade of white teeth, her irises, blue as the flower whose name she bore, were veiled in blonde lashes, and even Phil was dazzled. "Hmm... what's up with her?"

In an enclosure walled with hung fabric, Vinca served coffee. She was developing stiffly but efficiently, with a sort of acrobatic charm. When a gust of wind jostled the fragile table, Vinca used her foot to hold down a chair that threatened to overturn, her chin caught a lace napkin that was taking wing, without a break in her pouring an impeccable fount of coffee into a cup.

"Look at her!" the stranger gushed.

He called her a statuette, made her taste some chartreuse liqueur, asked her the names of the lovers whose hearts she had broken at the casino at Cancale.

"Ha! The casino at Cancale! There isn't any casino in Cancale!"

Vinca laughed, showed off the solid semicircle of her teeth, pivoted like a ballerina on the tips of her white shoes. She had cunning and flirtatiousness at her command; she didn't turn to look at Philippe. He contemplated her somberly from behind the piano and the huge bouquet of thistles planted in a copper bucket.

"I made a mistake," he confessed. "She's quite pretty. What do you know!"

When the phonograph started up, the stranger suggested to Vinca that she teach him the *balancello*, so Philippe slipped outside, ran to the beach, and tumbled into a hollow in the dunes, where he rested his head on his arms and his arms on his knees. A new Vinca, all voluptuous insolence, remained under his shut eyelids. Vinca the flirt, well-armed, suddenly enhanced by her rounded flesh, Vinca incredibly naughty and rebellious....

"Phil! My Phil! I was looking all over for you.... What's the matter?"

The seductress, panting, stood next to him, and ingenuously yanked a fistful of his hair to make him look up.

"Nothing," he said, his voice cracking.

He opened his eyes fearfully. Kneeling in the sand, she rumpled her ten organdy flounces, and crept toward him like a squaw.

"Phil! Come on, don't be mad.... You're holding something against me.... Phil, you know I care for you more than anyone else in the world. Talk to me, Phil!"

His eyes searched her for the ephemeral splendor that had so provoked him. But all that remained was a disheartened Vinca, an adolescent burdened too soon with the humiliation, the clumsiness, the mournful obstinacy of true love. He yanked back the hand she was kissing.

"Leave me alone! You don't understand, you never understand anything.... Come on, get up!"

And he attempted, by smoothing the rumpled dress, knotting the ribbon of her belt, calming the stiff hair that the wind had stood on end, he attempted to remold her in the shape of the little idol he had glimpsed.

"The vacation—at this point, it's only a matter of about a month and half!"

"A month," said Vinca. "You know very well I have to be back in Paris on September twentieth."

"Why is that? Your father is free till October first every year."

"Yes, but Mama and I, and Lisette, we don't have much time from September twentieth to October fourth to finish all the fall shopping; a school dress, a coat, a hat for me, and the same for Lisette...I mean, for us women...."

Lying on his back, Phil tossed fistfuls of sand into the air.

"Oh, so that's it! 'You women.' You're making a fuss just over that!"

"We have to. Your outfit is all there for you laid out on your bed. All you have to worry about is your shoes, since you buy them in a store that your father says you can't go to; the rest of it just sprouts up for you all by itself. How convenient for you men!"

Philippe plunked himself down, ready to respond to her sarcasm. But Vinca did not poke fun at him. She sewed, stitching a border of pink scallops for her crepon dress that matched the blue of her eyes. Her blonde hair, cut Joan-of-Arc style, was slowly growing out. She sometimes parted it at the nape of her neck, and tied it with blue ribbons into two short, wheat-colored brooms, resting against each cheek. Since lunch she had lost one of her ribbons, and half her hair, like a curtain unfurled, beat against half her face.

Philippe frowned:

"God, is your hair ever messy, Vinca!"

She blushed under her vacation sunburn and flashed him a humble look as she swept her hair back behind her ear:

"Oh, I know…My hair is going to be a mess so long as it's too short. In the meantime this hairstyle is…"

"Just temporary ugliness. It's all the same to you," he said, hard on her.

"I swear it's not, Phil."

Shamed by such sweetness, he fell silent, and she looked up, astonished, since she expected no indulgence from him. He himself believed it was only a temporary truce in her touchiness, and braced himself for her rebukes, her childish sarcasm, for what he called his young companion's "greyhound mood." But she smiled with a melancholy expression, a wandering smile that seemed meant for the calm sea, for the sky, where a high wind was sketching fern clouds.

"It's just the opposite, I really want to be pretty, I'm telling you. My mama says I still may be, but I need to have patience."

Her proud and awkward fifteen years had trained her for racing. Those years—salty, hardened, skinny, and solid—often made her like a brittle switch that lashed out, but her incomparable blue eyes, her simple and healthy mouth, were finished works of feminine grace.

"Patience, patience…."

Phil stood up, scraped the back of his espadrille against the dry dune, pearled with little empty snail shells. A word he detested had just poisoned the blissful siesta of his schoolboy vacation. This vigorous, sixteen-year-old had grown accustomed to idleness, to motionless languor, but the idea of waiting, of passive evolution, exasperated him. He clenched his fists, threw out his half-naked chest, challenged the horizon:

"Patience! That's the only word I ever hear out of any of you! You, your father, my teachers . . . God!"

Vinca put down her sewing to admire her companion's well-proportioned build, not distorted by adolescence. Brown hair, white skin, average height, he was growing slowly. From the age of fourteen he had resembled a little, well-built man, a bit taller every year.

"What else can I do, Phil? It's the only way. You always think you can throw your arms up and shout, 'God!' and it'll make something change. You think you're so much smarter than everyone but you'll show up for your baccalaureate exam just like the rest of them, and if you're lucky, you'll pass."

"Shut up!" he yelled. "You sound like my mother."

"And you sound like a little kid! What do you hope to accomplish, you poor thing, with all that impatience?"

Phil's dark eyes hated her for calling him, "you poor thing."

"I have no hope!" he declared tragically. "I certainly have no hope that you'll ever understand me! There you are, with your pink scallops, your back-to-school errands, your lessons, your little humdrum routine. . . . And me, all I've got is the idea that before long I'll be sixteen and a half. . . ."

Those periwinkle eyes, sparkling with tears of humiliation, managed to laugh:

"Oh, is that so? You think you're the King of the World, 'cause you're sixteen, is that it? Did you get that line from the movies?"

Phil grabbed her shoulder and shook her as if he owned her:

"I said shut up! Every time you open your mouth you say something stupid.... Don't you understand it's killing me, the idea that I'm only sixteen years old! These years ahead of me, the years of my baccalaureate exam, professional school, these years of groping, stuttering, where you have to start from scratch every time you fail, where you have to go over and over what you didn't get the first time.... These years where you have to seem to love a career, in front of Papa and Mama—just so you don't disappoint them, and you feel that they're beating their brains out just to look infallible, when they don't know any more about me than I do.... Don't you see, Vinca, I *loathe* this time in my life! Why can't I just be twenty-five right now and be done with the whole thing?"

He radiated intolerance and a sort of cultivated despair. His rush to grow old, his contempt for a time when the body and soul flourish, transformed this child of a minor Paris industrialist into a romantic hero. He fell down at Vinca's feet and continued his lament:

"So many more years, Vinca, when I'll just be almost a man, almost free, almost in love!"

She placed her hand on the black hair that the wind was folding back, level with Vinca's knees, and managed to possess all the womanly wisdom that was stirring in her. "Almost in love? So it's possible to be almost in love?"

Phil turned violently toward his friend. "So you claim you can put up with all this. Well, what are you planning to do?"

Faced with his black glance, she looked uncertain again:

"The same, Phil....I'm not going to pass my baccalaureate exam."

"Then what will you be? Have you decided if you're going to try industrial design? Or be a pharmacist?"

"Mama said..."

Without getting up he flung himself into a fury, like a colt:

"Oh, so 'Mama said,' did she!...You've got the makings of a great slave! And what *did* Mama say?"

"She said," repeated Vinca passively, "that she has rheumatism, that Lisette is only eight years old, and that without looking any farther I can find enough to do around our house, that soon I'll be keeping the books for our household, that I have to take charge of Lisette's education, the maids, all of it, in fact..."

"All of it! Nothing, nothing, and more nothing!"

"...that I'll get married..."

She blushed, her hand moved away from Philippe's hair, and she seemed to hope for a word that he did not utter.

"...In short, that until I get married, I have more than enough to keep me busy."

He turned around and looked her over disdainfully.

"And that's enough for you? That's enough for...let's see, five, six years, maybe more?"

Her blue eyes vacillated, but didn't swerve.

"Yes, Phil, while I'm waiting...since we're only fifteen and sixteen...since we don't have any choice but to wait."

He was shocked by that word he hated, and weakened by it. Once again the simplicity of his young companion and the submissiveness she confessed, that female manner of revering the ancient and modest household gods left him dumbfounded, disappointed, but vaguely appeased. Would he have accepted an exuberant Vinca, her nose turned toward the future, pawing the ground like a hobbled mare when faced with the long and hard passage of adolescence?

He leaned his head on his childhood friend's lap. Her slender knees trembled and closed, and Philippe dreamed, with sudden ardor, of the charming shape of those knees. But he shut his eyes, surrendered the trusting weight of his head, and rested there, waiting.

Phil was the first to reach the path—two ruts of dry sand, fluid as a wave, a rise between them sparsely covered with grass and corroded with salt—used by carts in the seaweed harvest, after spring tides. He leaned on the poles of the two nets and wore the two shrimp baskets bandoleered over his shoulder, but he had handed over to Vinca the two thin gaffs baited with raw fish and his fishing jacket, a precious rag with its sleeves amputated. He allowed himself a well-earned rest, and deigned to wait for his young, zealous friend, whom he had just left behind in a desert of rocks, pools, and seaweed that the August equinoctial tide had uncovered. His eyes searched for her before he slid down into the hollow of the road. At the foot of the sloping beach, among the fires of a hundred tiny mirrors of water where the sun flashed, a beret of blue wool, faded as a thistle in the dunes, marked the spot where Vinca, obstinate, was still hunting for shrimp and rosy hermit crabs.

"If it makes her happy! ..." said Philippe under his breath.

He let himself slide into the rut of cool sand and deliciously molded his naked torso to it. By his head he could hear the humid rustling of a handful of shrimp in the baskets, and the claws of a large crab scraping purposefully against the lid.

Philippe sighed, overcome by a vague and unblemished happiness, mixing together his agreeable fatigue, the vibration of his muscles still taut from the climb, and the hues and heat of a Brittany afternoon heavy with a salty mist. He sat down, his eyes dazzled by the milky sky they had contemplated and was surprised to see again the fresh bronze of his legs, of his arms— arms and legs of a sixteen-year-old, thin, but with a full shape that the dry muscle had not yet emerged from, and which could inflate the pride of a girl as much as a young man. With his hand he wiped his ankle, which was bleeding, flayed, and licked off his hand the blood and the sea water mingling their salt.

The breeze blowing off the land smelled of the newly mown hay, the stables, crushed peppermint; a dusty pink, level with the sea, was slowly taking the place of the immutable blue that had reigned since morning. Philippe did not know how to say to himself, "There are only a few hours in life when a contented body, with its eyes rewarded for their efforts, and a heart—light, resonating, almost empty—receive in one moment all that they are capable of containing, and I will remember this." Instead, all it took was a cracked bell and the voice of the kid goat who was swinging it around its neck to make the corners of his mouth quake with worry, and pleasure fill his eyes with tears. He did not turn to look at the wet rocks his friend was wandering over, and his pure emotion never breathed the name Vinca; to rescue an unhoped-for delight, a sixteen-year-old child cannot call on another child, perhaps similarly overloaded.

"You! Boy!"

The voice that roused him was young, authoritarian. Phil turned around without getting up, and saw a lady dressed all in white ten steps away from him, plunging her white high heels and her walking stick into the seaweed road.

"Tell me, boy, I can't take my car any farther down this road, can I?"

Out of politeness Philippe got up, approached her, and only blushed once he was standing, once he felt on his naked torso the cooling wind and the glance of that lady in white, who smiled and changed her tone of voice.

"Excuse me, Monsieur... I'm certain my chauffeur made a wrong turn. I tried to warn him.... This road dead ends in a footpath and only leads down to the sea, doesn't it?"

"Yes, Madame. It's the seaweed road."

"The Seaweed Road? And how far is it to Seaweed?"

Phil did not have time to hold in a burst of laughter that the lady in white good-naturedly echoed:

"Oh! Did I say something amusing? Watch out, you're going to make me speak to you like a grown-up to a child; you seem twelve years old when you laugh."

But she looked him right in the eye as if he were a man.

"Madame, the seaweed isn't *Seaweed*, it's... it's just seaweed."

"An illuminating explanation," allowed the lady in white, "and one for which I'm most obliged."

She bantered in a manly way, condescending, just like her calm glance, and Philippe suddenly felt tired, teetering and weak, paralyzed by one of those crises of femininity that possesses an adolescent face to face with a woman.

"And did you catch many fish, Monsieur?"

"No, Madame, not many...I mean...Vinca has more shrimp than me...."

"Who is Vinca? Your sister?"

"No, Madame, she's a friend."

"Vinca...A foreign name?"

"No...yes, it means Periwinkle."

"Someone your age?"

"She's fifteen. I'm sixteen."

"Sixteen..." repeated the lady all in white.

She refrained from commenting on this, and added a moment later:

"You've got sand on your cheek."

He wiped his cheek in a frenzy, almost flaying his skin, then his arm fell to his side. *I can't feel my arms any more,* he thought. *I think I'm going to be sick....*

The lady all in white released Philippe from her calm gaze and smiled:

"Here's Vinca now," she said, pointing to the bend in the road where the girl appeared, hauling a wood frame net and Philippe's jacket. "Goodbye, Monsieur—"

"Phil," he said automatically.

She did not extend her hand and said farewell with a nod of her head that she repeated two or three times, like a woman responding, "Yes, yes," to a hidden thought. She was not yet out of sight when Vinca ran up to him.

"Phil! What's with that woman?"

With his shoulders and the expression on his face he tried to say that he knew nothing about it.

"You don't know her and you talked to her?"

Phil looked his girlfriend over with a malice that suddenly reared up again, a malice that shook off a momentary yoke. He thought pleasantly about their age, their friendship—already riled—his own despotism, and Vinca's surly devotion. Wringing wet, she had the bruised knees of Saint Sebastian, perfect under their scarred epidermis; the hands of a gardener's assistant or a cabin boy; a handkerchief turned green formed a cravat at her neck, and her blouse smelled of raw mussels. Her nappy old beret no longer struggled against the blue of her eyes, and apart from her worried, jealous, eloquent eyes, she looked like a high school boy wearing a disguise. Phil started to laugh and Vinca stamped her foot, throwing his blazer back in his face:

"Would you answer me?"

Nonchalantly he slipped his naked arms into the empty armholes of the jacket.

"Go away, you fool! It's a lady with a car who's lost. A little farther and the car would've gotten stuck here. I gave her directions."

"Oh...."

Vinca sat down and emptied out her espadrilles. Wet gravel rained from them.

"So why did she leave so suddenly, just when I was about to get here?"

Philippe took his time before answering. Once again, in secret, he savored the deliberate self-assurance, the steady glance of the unknown woman, and her meditative smile. He remembered that she had called him "monsieur" quite seriously. But he also remembered that she had said "Vinca" brusquely, in a manner that was altogether too familiar—even insulting. He wrinkled his eyebrows and his look protected his friend's innocent confusion. His mind roamed for a moment and came up with an ambiguous answer that satisfied both his taste for this romantic secret and his prudishness as a young bourgeois:

"She did right," he replied.

He tried pleading with her:

"Vinca? Look at me! Give me your hand.... Let's talk about something else."

She turned away from him, toward the window, and gently pulled back her hand:

"Leave me alone. I'm feeling blue."

The August equinoctial tide, bringing the rain, filled the

ow. The land ended there, at the hem of the sandy field. One

e push by the wind, one more rise in the ploughed gray field
of parallel lines of foam, and the house would, no doubt, sail off
like an ark.... But Phil and Vinca knew the August tide and its
monotonous thunder, the September tide and its disheveled
white horses. They knew that the edge of this meadow would
remain unbreachable, and their youth had scoffed every year at
the soapy lashings that danced, impotent, at the nibbled edges of
humanity's empire.

Phil reopened the glass door, closed it again with difficulty,
turned his face to the wind and tilted his forehead back into the
fine rain, winnowed out by the storm, the sweet sea rain, a bit
salty, that traveled through the air like smoke. On the lawn he
gathered up the bocci balls studded with steel and the boxwood
jack, left out that morning, the tambourine-shaped racquets and
the rubber balls. In the shed he arranged these toys that he no
longer enjoyed, as one arranges the elements of a disguise that
has to last for a long time. Behind the window, periwinkle eyes
followed him, and the drops sliding along the glass seemed to
stream from her anxious eyes, their blue deriving neither from the
marbled pewter of the sky nor the verdigris of the leaden sea.

Phil folded up the wooden chairs, tilted up the rattan table.
He didn't toss a casual smile at his girlfriend. It had been a long
time since they had needed smiles to please each other, and
nothing today pulled them toward joy.

Green Wheat

A few more days, three weeks, Phil said to himself. He wiped the sand off his hands on a clump of moist wild thyme, laden with flowers and little hornets trapped by the rain, who waited numbly for the next ray of sun. He breathed on his palms the chaste, fresh perfume, and resisted a wave of weakness, of sweetness, of the sadness of a ten-year-old child. But he saw leaning against the glass, between the long tears of the rain and the swirling corollas of the rumpled morning-glories, Vinca's face, a woman's face that she showed only to him; a face she hid behind her girlish, reasonable, and happy fifteen years.

A swatch of clear sky held the downpour up in the clouds, half-opened above the horizon a luminous wound. From that wound spread an inverted fan of sunbeams in a sad hue of white. Philippe's soul shot out to meet that break, in quest of the kindness, the ease that his tormented sixteen years naively claimed. But facing the sea, he felt the shut window at his back and Vinca pressing up against the glass.

A few more days, he repeated to himself, *and we'll be apart. What can I do?*

He was not even thinking that the end of the vacation the year before had made him unhappy, but his return to Paris and school had calmed him down, and he had resigned himself to Sunday consolations. The year before, Philippe was fifteen; each birthday shut away, into a troubled and miserable past, all that was not part of Vinca and him. *Do I love her that much?* he asked himself, and finding no word other than love, he furiously tossed his hair back.

Maybe it's not because I love her that much, but because she belongs to me. That's it!

He turned back toward the house and yelled into the wind:

"Vinca! Come out, the rain's stopped!"

She opened the door and stood on the threshold like someone ill, fearfully raising a shoulder almost to her ear.

"Come on, let's go! The tide is going out again, it'll push back the rain!"

She tied her hair up with a white scarf knotted at the nape, which made her look wounded.

"At least come as far as The Nose, the rocks are dry."

Without uttering a word she followed him along the customs officers' path, on a ledge running along the side of a cliff. They crushed peppered marjoram underfoot and the last scent of sweet clover. Below them, the sea clapped its torn flags and unctuously licked the rocks. Its force pushed warm whiffs of air to the top of the cliff, bearing the odor of mussels and the earthy aromas of the little niches where the wind and birds sowed seeds in their flight.

They arrived at their hideout—it was dry, well sheltered under a prow of rocks, an eyrie without a ledge where they seemed to sail out onto the high seas. Philippe sat down next to Vinca, who rested her head on his shoulder. She seemed worn out and immediately shut her eyes. Her cheeks, brown, pink, and round, sandy with russet grains, velvet with a downy vegetal softness, had grown pale since morning, as had her moist mouth, always a bit cracked like a fruit bitten by the day's heat.

After lunch, instead of countering the complaints of her "childhood sweetheart" with the usual good sense of an intelligent, stubborn, and sweet middle-class girl, she had burst into tears, made desperate confessions, bitterly announcing how much she hated their youth, their unattainable future, the impossibility of eloping, the unacceptability of resignation. She shouted: "I love you!" the way one shouts, "Farewell!" and, "I can't leave you ever again!" with eyes filled with horror. Love, which had grown larger before their eyes, had touched their childhood with magic and protected their adolescence from questionable friendships. Less ignorant than Daphnis, Philippe had treated Vinca roughly and with reverence, like a brother, but also cherished her as if they had been, as in the Orient, married in their cradles.

Vinca sighed, opened her eyes again without looking up:

"Am I wearing you out, Phil?"

He indicated that she wasn't, admiring, so close to his, her blue eyes whose blue, each time dearer to his heart, fluttered between her blonde-tipped lashes.

"See," he pointed, "the storm's coming. It'll be high tide again at four in the morning.... But we'll have a clearing and this evening the moon will be full when it rises."

Instinctively he spoke of a break in the weather, of calming, to lead Vinca toward images of serenity. But she didn't respond.

"Are you going to come play tennis tomorrow at the Jallons' house?"

She shook her head No with a sudden fury, her eyes closed, as if she had permanently refused to drink, to eat, to live.

"Vinca!" pleaded Philippe sternly. "We have to. We're going."

She half opened her mouth, directed her glance at the sea with the look of someone condemned to death:

"Then we're going," she repeated. "What's the use of not going? What's the use of going? Nothing will change anything."

They both were thinking about the Jallons' garden, about tennis, about the afternoon snack they would have there. They were both thinking, pure and furious lovers that they were, about the game that would disguise them again tomorrow as laughing children, and they felt exhausted.

Only a few more days, Philippe said to himself, *and we'll be separated. We won't wake up any more under the same roof, and I'll see Vinca only on Sundays, at her father's, or at mine, or at the movies. And I'm sixteen. Sixteen plus five twenty-one. Hundreds, hundreds of days . . . A few months of vacation, true, but the end is horrible . . . and yet she's mine . . . she's mine. . . .*

Then he realized that Vinca was sliding off his shoulder. With a soft, imperceptible, intentional gesture she was sliding, with her eyes closed, down the slope of the rocky plateau, so narrow that Vinca's feet were already dangling over the void. He understood and didn't shudder. He weighed the advisability of what his friend was attempting, and locked his arm around Vinca's stomach, so he could not lose hold of her. Pressing her against him, he felt the living reality, the elasticity, the vigorous perfection of the young woman's body ready to obey him in life, ready to drag him with her to their death.

Die? What for?... Not yet. Do we have to set out for the next world without really having all of this, which was made for me?

On this slanting rock, he dreamed of possession the way a shy adolescent would, but also the way a demanding man would, an heir bitterly resolved to enjoy those goods for which time and human law had destined him. For the first time, it was he alone who was deciding their fate as a couple, master of the choice of abandoning her to the sea or snatching her from the rocky ledge, like the stubborn seed, though nourished on so little, that still bloomed there.

He hoisted her up, tightening his arms like a belt around the graceful body that was limp and heavy, and roused his friend with a quick summons:

"Vinca! C'mon!"

She contemplated him standing above her, saw how resolute, how impatient he was, and understood that the moment for death had passed. With rapturous indignation she found again the rays of the sunset in Philippe's black eyes, his disheveled hair, his mouth, and the wing-shaped shadow of virile down on his lips, and she shouted:

"You don't love me enough, Phil, you don't love me enough!"

He wanted to say something, and he was silent, since he had no noble confession to make. He blushed and bowed his head, guilty—when she had slid toward the place where love no longer torments its victims before their time—of having treated his friend as an unclaimed object, precious and sealed, whose secret alone was important—and of having refused to give Vinca to Death.

For several days the scent of fall had drifted down as far as the sea.

From dawn till the hour when the warmed earth allowed the fresh breath of the sea to push back the aroma, less dense, of open furrows, of threshed wheat, of steaming manure, those August mornings smelled like fall. A tenacious dew sparkled at the foot of the hedges, and if at noontime Vinca gathered up an aspen leaf, ripe and fallen before its time, the white underside of the still-green leaf was damp and sprinkled with diamonds. Moist mushrooms popped up from the earth, and because of the cooler nights, spiders in the gardens returned in the evening to the shed where the games were kept, and neatly arranged themselves on the ceiling.

But the middle of the days escaped both the net of the autumn fog and the gossamer stretched across the brambles weighted with mulberries—the season seemed to retrace its steps back to July. At the zenith of the sky, the sun drank up the dew, putrefied the newborn mushrooms, riddled the aged vineyards and their stunted grapes with wasps, and Vinca and Lisette, with one gesture, shucked off the light knit jackets that since breakfast had protected their arms and their naked necks, brown beyond their white dresses. Then came a succession of motionless days, without wind or clouds, except the milky, meandering whispy cattails of cirrus that appeared around midday and vanished: days so divinely similar one to the next that Vinca and Philippe, soothed, might have believed the year had stopped at its sweetest moment, softly shackled by an August that would never end.

Overcome with physical happiness, they thought less about their separation in September and left behind their dramas of adolescents already grown old. At fifteen and sixteen they were already worn out by a premature love, by secrets, silence, and the periodic bitterness of their separations.

A few of their young neighbors, with whom they played tennis and went fishing, had already left the seaside for Touraine; the villas closest to them were shuttered; Philippe and Vinca were alone on the coast, in the big house whose polished-wood entrance hall smelled like a boat. They tasted perfect solitude in the midst of the parents they brushed by at all hours of the day but barely saw. Vinca, preoccupied with Philippe, still fulfilled all the duties required of a young woman—gathered viburnum and shaggy clematis from the garden to place on the table; culled from the kitchen garden the first pears and the last of the black currants; she served the coffee; lit matches for her father, for Philippe's father; sewed and seamed little dresses for Lisette; and lived, among the phantom parents whom she hardly paid attention to and barely heard, a strange life; among them she endured the pleasant, half-deaf, half-blind beginnings of a dizzy spell. Her younger sister Lisette was still immune to the common fate and shone with pure and veracious color. Lisette resembled "Periwinkle" like a little mushroom resembles a larger mushroom.

"If I die," Vinca said to Philippe, "you'll still have Lisette."

But Philippe shrugged his shoulders and refused to laugh, since sixteen-year-olds in love do not admit the possibility of change, sickness, or infidelity, and leave room for death in their plans only if they perceive it as a reward or use it as a way to unravel their fate, the only one that seemed possible.

On the most beautiful morning in August, Phil and Vinca decided to skip the family meal and bring along a picnic basket fastened to their waists, containing their lunch and their bathing suits; and Lisette. In years past, they had often had lunch by themselves, like explorers, in the hollows of the cliffs; a worn-out pleasure, a pleasure now spoiled by worry and doubts. But this most beautiful morning made even these strayed children feel younger, since they sometimes looked back longingly at the invisible door to their lost childhood. Philippe went ahead along the customs officers' path, carrying the nets for the afternoon's fishing and the string bearing the bonging liter of foamy cider and the bottle of mineral water. Lisette, in a knit top and bathing suit, swung the warm bread knotted in a napkin, and Vinca brought up the rear, in a blue sweater and white shorts, bearing baskets like an African mule. In the tricky spots, Philippe shouted without turning around:

"Hold on, I'll take one of the baskets!"

"Don't bother," answered Vinca.

And she found a way to guide Lisette, when the high ferns submerged her little head and her skull-cap of stiff, blonde hair.

They chose their cove, a fault in the rocks that the tides had provided with fine sand. It spread out to the sea in a cornucopia. Lisette took off her sandals and played with empty shells. Vinca rolled her white shorts up her brown thighs and dug out the moist sand under a rock, to rest the bottles in a cool spot.

"Do you want any help?" Philippe suggested softly.

She did not deign to answer and looked at him with a silent laugh. The rare blue of her eyes, her cheeks tanned to a hot rouge like espaliered nectarines, the curved, two-edged blade of her teeth shone for a moment with inexpressibly powerful color that hit Philippe like a wound. But she turned away, and he watched her calmly going, coming, and deftly bending down, as free of inhibitions and clothes as a young man.

"Oh, I know all you brought along was your hungry mouth!" shouted Vinca. "Men!"

This "man," all of sixteen years old, accepted the teasing and the compliment. He called Lisette sternly when the food was ready, ate the sandwiches his friend buttered for him, drank the pure cider, drenched in salt the lettuce and the Gruyère dice, licked the moisture of the luscious pears from his lips. Vinca watched it all like a young cup-bearer, her forehead circled by a blue headband. She removed the bones from the sardines for Lisette, portioned out the drinks, peeled the fruits, then ate quickly, with big chomps of her fine set of teeth. The tide, going out, whispered softly a few meters away; a threshing machine buzzed above them along the coast, and the nearby rocks, with their beards of grass and little yellow blossoms, oozed unsalted water that smelled of the earth.

Philippe lay down, an arm folded behind his head.

"Beautiful day," he murmured.

Vinca stood up, her hands busy wiping off the knives and glasses, and let the blue rays of her glance fall on him. He didn't move, hiding the pleasure he felt when his friend admired him. At that moment he knew he was handsome, his cheeks warm, his mouth lustrous, his forehead framed by the harmonious disorder of his black hair.

Without a word Vinca resumed the duties of a young squaw and Philippe shut his eyes, lulled by the ebb flow, a faraway chime sounding noon, the song Lisette sang under her breath. A quick and light sleep descended over him, a siesta pierced by every noise, but making use of each noise in his tenacious dream: lying on that blonde coast after having eaten a child's picnic, he was at the same time ancient and savage Phil, stripped of everything, but primitively gratified, since he was possessing a woman.

A louder cry forced him to raise his eyelids; by the sea that the noontime glare and the vertical light drained of its color, Vinca, leaning against Lisette, was tending to a minor wound. Vinca confidently pulled out a thorn with a small, raised hand. This picture did not trouble Philippe's daydream, and he shut his eyes again.

A child... that's it, we have a child....

His virile dream, where a precocious love let itself be overtaken by its simple and unselfish destiny, dove toward solitudes where he was the master. He passed by a grotto—a hammock of fibers with a naked shape sinking into it, a glowing red fire that beat its wings level with the ground—then lost his oracular sense, his power to fly, capsized, and touched the luxurious depths of the blackest repose.

"It's unbelievable how short the days are getting!"

"Why unbelievable? You say the same thing this time every year. You can't change the solstice, Marthe."

"Who was talking about the solstice? I don't expect anything from the solstice; I don't think it wants anything from me, either."

"I've always marveled at the inability of women to master certain forms of knowledge. Twenty times I've explained to this woman how the tides work, and it's like talking to a wall when I mention syzygies!"

"Auguste, it's not because you're my brother-in-law that I listen to you more than the others...."

"Lord! It no longer amazes me that you're not married, Marthe. Nudge my wife to pass me the ashtray, please."

"If I pass it to you, where do you think Audebert is going to put the ashes from his pipe?"

"Madame Ferret, don't trouble yourself over that, the children have scattered abalone shells over every table."

"It's your fault, Audebert. That day you said to them, 'Those abalone shells are so pretty. They'd make artistic ashtrays,' you turned their wandering on the rocks into a secret mission. Isn't that so, Phil?"

"Yes, Monsieur Ferret."

"It's because of that mission that your daughter gave up her first commercial venture, Ferret. Vinca thought up the idea—do you know what she did?—of cutting a deal with Carbonieux, a major dealer in birds and seeds, to supply him with the cuttlefish bones that caged canaries sharpen their beaks on! Go on, tell them, Vinca, am I lying?"

"No, Monsieur Audebert."

"She has more business sense than we give her credit for, the little rascal. I sometimes regret..."

"Oh, Auguste! Don't start that again!"

"I'll say it again if I want. Here's a child you say you'd like to keep at home. Fine. What grist are you going to give her for her mental and physical activity?"

"The same as I give myself. You don't see me twiddling my thumbs, do you? And besides, I'm going to marry her off. Period, end of sentence."

"My sister believes in the ancient traditions."

"I don't see husbands complaining about them."

"Well said, Madame Ferret. A girl's future...I know there's no hurry. Fifteen years old...Vinca has plenty of time to find her calling. Isn't that so, Vinca? Did you hear me? What says the accused in her own defense?"

"Nothing, Monsieur Audebert."

"'Nothing, Monsieur Audebert!' Now you're chewing your nails. Our children are good at making fun of us, Ferret! And they're strangely quiet tonight."

"They live a madcap life. You might say Vinca has worn the bottom out of her fishing shorts."

"Marthe!"

"Marthe what? All I said was 'shorts'! We're not English, after all!"

"In front of a nice young man!"

"He's not a nice young man, he's Phil. What are you drawing, Phil, m'boy?"

"A turbine engine, Monsieur Ferret."

"My compliments to the future engineer.... Audebert, have you seen the moon over Le Grouin? I've been looking at that August moon rise over the sea for fifteen summers now, and I never get tired of it. When you think that fifteen years ago, Le Grouin was naked, and that it was the wind that sowed all those bushes...."

"You're talking to me like I'm some kind of tourist, Ferret! Fifteen years ago I was looking for a corner along the coast where I could salt away the first six hundred I'd been able to put aside...."

"Is it fifteen years already! It's true, Philippe wasn't even walking yet.... Honey, come look at the moon and tell me if you've ever seen it that color these fifteen years? It's...God, it's green! Absolutely green!"

Philippe raised his inquisitive eyes to Vinca. They had just evoked a time when she hadn't appeared yet, but she was already somewhat alive.... Though he had no definite memories of that period when they stumbled together on the blonde sand of their vacations, that little shape of ages ago, white muslin and browned flesh, had dissolved. But when he said in his heart of hearts: *Vinca!* the name brought back, inseparable from his friend, the memory of the sand, warm on his knees, squeezed tight and leaking out of his palms....

Periwinkle eyes met those of Philippe, and finding his equally opaque, quickly darted away.

"Vinca, aren't you going upstairs to bed?"

"Not just yet, Mama, please. I'm finishing the large scallop on that one-piece outfit of Lisette's."

She spoke sweetly, then flung far away from her and Philippe the pale Shadows that were barely there, the Shadows that made up the family circle. Phil, having drawn his turbine engine, the propeller of a plane, the mechanism of a separator, added to the blades of his propeller the large, shadowy eyes of a peacock butterfly, a few delicate paws, and antennae. Then he traced a capital V, and changed its shape with the help of a blue pencil until it resembled an azure eye, bordered by long lashes—Vinca's eye.

"Look, Vinca."

She leaned over, placed on the paper her Amazon hand, brown as hardwood, and smiled:

"Oh, you're so silly!"

"What did he do now?" exclaimed Monsieur Audebert.

The two young people turned toward the voice, looking astonished and slightly haughty.

"Nothing, Papa," said Philippe. "Stupid things. I put paws on my turbine engine so it could run better."

"When you reach the age of reason, it'll be a red letter day, all right. He isn't sixteen, the boy is more like six years old!"

Vinca and Philippe smiled politely, and banished again from their presence those hazy beings who played cards or embroidered near them. They still heard, as if above gurgling water, a few jokes about Phil's "calling," betrothed to mechanics and applied electronics, about Vinca's marriage, a familiar refrain. Laughter rose up from the dining room table, because someone had spoken of uniting Philippe and Vinca.

"Uh uh, it'd be like a sister and brother marrying! They know each other too well."

"Love, Madame Ferret, desires the unexpected, the lightning bolt!"

"Love is a gypsy child. . . ."

"Marthe! Don't sing! You'll drive away our northwest wind and the beautiful weather, and we just got them back!"

Vinca engaged to him? Philippe smiled, full of condescension and pity. Engaged . . . what for? Vinca belonged to him, just as he belonged to Vinca. They had wisely anticipated just how an official engagement, which they were so far from being able to bring to fruition, would disturb their long passion. They had predicted the daily teasing, the intolerable laughter, and also the distrust.

Entrenched in their love, they shut the peephole through which they sometimes communicated with real life. They also

envied their parents' childishness, their easy laughter, their faith in
a peaceful future.

They're so carefree! Philippe said to himself. He searched his
father's gray forehead for a trace of light, or at least a burn. *Well,*
he declared to himself in a superior manner, *the poor guy has never
been in love. . . .*

Vinca made an effort to summon up a time when her mother,
a young girl, may have suffered from love and silence. She saw the
prematurely white hair, the gold pince-nez, and the svelte figure
that made Madame Ferret such a distinguished woman.

Vinca blushed, feeling again both her own shame in love, and
the torment of the body and soul. She left behind those vain
Shadows in order to rejoin Phil on a path where they hid their
tracks and felt they might die if they carried away spoils that
were too heavy, too rich, and plundered too soon.

At a bend in a narrow road, Phil jumped down onto the chalky
grass on the slope, throwing his bicycle to one side and his body
to the other.

Enough, enough! I'm dying. Why did I ever volunteer to deliver this telegram?

The eleven kilometers from their villa to Saint-Malo hadn't
seemed too hard to him. The sea breeze pushed him forward, and
the two long downhill stretches pressed against his half-naked

chest a sash of fresh, restless air. But the trip back made him lose
his taste for summer, cycling, and doing favors. August was going
down in flames. Philippe plunked his two feet onto the yellow
grass and licked from his lips the fine dust of the siliceous roads.
He fell onto his back with his arms crossed. A temporary con-
gestion drew dark circles under his eyes as if he had just climbed
out of a boxing ring, and his two bronzed legs, naked below his
racing shorts, provided a tally, in white scars, in black or red
wounds, of his weeks of vacation and his days spent fishing along
the rocky coast.

"I should've brought Vinca," he snickered. "She'd be crooning
all sorts of complaints now!"

But another Philippe within him, the Philippe who was
smitten with Vinca, the Philippe who was shut inside his
precocious love like an orphan prince in a cavernous palace,
answered the bad Philippe: "You would've carried her on your
back as far as the villa, if she'd grumbled."

"Not necessarily," protested the bad Philippe. And this time
the Philippe who was in love did not dare argue with the other.

He stretched out at the foot of a wall crowned by blue pines,
white aspens. Philippe had known the coast by heart ever since he
could walk on two feet and ride on two wheels. *That's Ker-Anna. I*
hear the generator that runs the lights. I wonder who rented the estate this
summer? A motor, behind the wall, seemed from a distance like
the clicking tongue of a panting dog, and the leaves of the silver

aspens were brushed back by the wind like wavelets in a channel. Phil closed his eyes.

"It seems to me you've earned yourself a glass of orangeade, Monsieur Phil," said a calm voice.

Phil, opening his eyes, saw a woman's face leaning over him, reversed as in a mirror of water. This face, upside-down, had a somewhat fleshy chin, a mouth intensified by lipstick, a nose with pinched, irritable nostrils, and two dark eyes that, seen from below, formed two crescents. Her whole face, the color of light amber, smiled in a way that was familiar but hardly friendly. Philippe recognized the lady in white, bogged down with her car on the seaweed road, the woman who had questioned him by first calling him, "Hey, boy!" and then, "Monsieur." He sprang to his feet and greeted her as best he could. She leaned against her crossed arms, bare except for her white dress, and looked him over from head to toe, as she had done the first time.

"Monsieur," she inquired seriously, "is it because of some vow you've taken, or is it just by choice that you never wear clothes, or hardly any?"

Philippe's cooled blood surged up to his ears, to his cheeks, where it started to burn again.

"No, Madame," he protested bitterly, "it's because I had to bring a message to the telegraph office that my father was sending to a client; no one else in the house was about to do it; he couldn't send Vinca or Lisette in weather like this!"

"Don't make a scene," said the Lady in White. "I'm terribly impressionable. Any little thing can make me dissolve into tears."

Her words, her opaque look that slowly grew into a wry smile, wounded Philippe. He grabbed his bicycle by the handlebars, the way one would jerk the arm of a child who had fallen down, and started to climb back on.

"Have a glass of orangeade, Monsieur Phil. I insist."

He heard the grating of an iron grill at an angle to the wall, and his attempt to escape led him right to an open door, to a path of apoplectic pink hydrangeas, and to the Lady in White.

"My name is Madame Dalleray," she said.

"Philippe Audebert," blurted Phil.

She made a sketchy gesture of indifference and said, "Oh!..." meaning: "That's of no interest to me."

She walked alongside him, not bothered by the heat of the sun on her hair—black, pulled back, and shining. His head began to ache, and he felt a touch of sunstroke as he rediscovered in Madame Dalleray's presence that hope, that apprehension of a swoon that would deliver him from thinking, choosing, and obeying.

"Totote! Some orangeade!" called Madame Dalleray.

Phil trembled, suddenly awake: *The wall is over there,* he said to himself. *It's not too high. I could just jump over it and...* He stopped himself from finishing his thought with, *... and I'll be saved.* Following the white dress, he scaled the dazzling steps of the entrance. He summoned all the insolence of his sixteen years: *Well, she won't eat me alive!... If it means so much to her not to waste her orangeade!...*

He went inside and felt over his head as soon as he penetrated a black room, bolted against rays of light and flies. The low temperature that the closed shutters and curtains maintained took his breath away. His foot banged against a soft piece of furniture, he fell on a cushion, heard a small, demonic laugh coming from an unknown direction, and he almost burst into nervous tears. A frosted glass touched his hand.

"Don't gulp it down all at once," said the voice of Madame Dalleray. "Totote, that was crazy to put ice in it. The cellar is cold enough."

A white hand dipped three fingers into the glass and immediately pulled them out. The fire of a diamond was shining, reflected in the ice cube clenched by three fingers. With his throat clenched tight and his eyes closed, Philippe drank two sips. He did not even taste the acid flavor of the orange; but when he raised his eyelids, his eyes, now used to the dark, made out the red and white of a tapestry, the muted black and gold of the curtains. A woman, whom he had not seen, disappeared, carrying a tinkling tray. A red and blue macaw on its perch opened one wing with the sound of a fan, revealing its armpit, the color of aroused flesh.

"He's beautiful," said Phil, his voice cracking.

"Even more because he's mute," said Madame Dalleray.

She had sat down far away from Phil. From a chalice, a vertical

47

plume of burning fragrance rose up between them, spreading an odor of resin and geraniums. Phil crossed his naked legs, and the Lady in White smiled, heightening the sensation of a sumptuous nightmare, an arbitrary custody, an equivocal kidnapping that swept away all of Philippe's composure.

"Your parents come to the seashore every year, don't they?" finally said the sweet, virile voice of Madame Dalleray.

"Yes," he sighed despondently.

"Well, I find this area quite charming, and I didn't know it at all before coming here. A Brittany with moderation, not particularly characteristic, but restful, and the color of the sea here is incomparable."

Philippe didn't answer. He devoted the remainder of his lucidity to his gradual exhaustion, and expected to hear his blood dripping onto the rug—the regular, muffled, last drops leaving his heart.

"But for you it's love, isn't it?"

"For who?" he said with a start.

"The coast here at Cancale, right?"

"Yes...."

"Monsieur Phil, you're not in pain, are you? No? Good. Though I'm a very good nurse.... But in this weather you're absolutely right, it's better to keep still than to talk. Let's be still."

"I didn't say that...."

She hadn't moved at all since they had entered the dark room, nor had she risked one word that wasn't completely banal. Yet the sound of her voice, each time, inexplicably traumatized Phil, and the threat of a mutual silence terrified him. His exit was pitiful and desperate. He banged his glass against a phantom side table, uttered a few words he himself didn't hear, stood up, reached the door by breaking through heavy waves and invisible obstacles, and when he found the light again he breathed as if he had almost been asphyxiated.

"Ah!..." he said half out loud.

And he pressed, with a pathetic hand, the spot on his breast where we believe the heart beats.

Then he brusquely regained his awareness of reality, laughed foolishly, cavalierly shook Madame Dalleray's hand, grabbed his bicycle, and left. At the top of the last hill he found Vinca, worried, waiting for him:

"What were you doing all this time, Phil?"

Through eyelids blued by her pupils, he kissed his girlfriend's charming eyes, and answered over-enthusiastically:

"What was I doing? What do you think? Everything! I was ambushed going around a bend, held prisoner in a cave, dosed with powerful drugs, tied naked to a post, whipped, interrogated."

Vinca laughed, leaning on his shoulder, while Philippe shook his head to flick two nervous tears off his eyelashes, and he thought:

If she only knew how true that really is.

Colette

Ever since Madame Dalleray had offered him a glass of orangeade, Phil had felt on his lips and at the back of his throat the shock, the burning of that icy drink. It seemed to him that never in his life had he drunk, or would ever drink again, an orangeade that bitter.

But at the time I was drinking it, I didn't even taste it.... It was only afterward...long afterward.... That visit, which he hid from Vinca, formed a dot in his memory, a beating and sensitive dot, whose benign fever he could speed up or calm, according to his fancy.

Philippe's life still belonged to Vinca, the girl of his heart, born near him, twelve months after him, attached to him like a twin to her brother, anxious as a lover who tomorrow must lose her mate. But neither dreams nor nightmares are dependent on real life. A bad dream, rich in glacial shadows, in muted reds, in black and gold velvet, encroached on Phil's life, and like the phases of an eclipse, it had shrunk the normal hours of daylight ever since that torrid afternoon in that living room at Ker-Anna when he had drunk the glass of orangeade poured by the imperious and solemn Lady in White. The fire of the diamond at the edge of the glass...the ice cubes, like dice, sparkling among three pale fingers...the blue and red macaw, mute on its perch, its wing lined with white plumage, rosy as the flesh of peaches....

The boy doubted his memory when he sifted again through these images with their fiery and false colors, a stage set created perhaps by sleep, which pushes the green of foliage as far as blue and imbues certain nuances with emotion.

That visit had yielded no pleasure for him. The very memory of that fragrant smoke from the chalice once paralyzed his appetite, caused his nerves to go off kilter:

"Vinca! Doesn't the shrimp smell like benzoin today?"

Pleasure, to enter the sealed room, to grope among soft and velvety obstacles? Pleasure, his clumsy escape, the sun suddenly bearing down on his shoulders? No, no, nothing about it resembled pleasure, it was more like uneasiness, being tormented by a debt....

"I owe her a favor," Philippe told himself one morning. "There's nothing that says I have to be rude to her. I should leave some flowers at her doorstep, and then I'll be done with it. But what flowers?"

The China asters of the vegetable garden and velvety snapdragons seemed contemptible to him. The end of August had deflowered the wild honeysuckle and the Dorothy Perkinses scrolling around the trunks of the aspens. But a hollow in the dunes between the villa and the sea—filled to the edges with sea holly and its blue flowers, mauve the length of their brittle stems—deserved to be called "the mirror of Vinca's eyes."

"Sea holly...I saw some in a copper vase at Madame

Dalleray's.... Does one give sea holly? I'll hang them on the gate.... I won't go in...."

With the wisdom of his sixteen years he waited for the day when Vinca, tired, a bit ill, droopy and snappish, a mauve margin under her blue eyes, stretched out in the shade, refusing to go for a swim or a walk. Secretly he clipped and bundled the most beautiful sea holly, madly tearing his hands on their iron foliage. He took off on his bicycle, on a mild Brittany day that veiled the earth with mist and mixed an intangible milk into the sea. He pedaled, bothered by his white canvas pants and his thickest, handsomest jacket, to the walls of Ker-Anna, walked bent over toward the gate and wanted to throw his bunch of flowers into the garden, as if to get rid of the evidence. He thought about just how he would make this gesture, spotted the place where the surrounding walls almost touched the villa, made a catapult of his arm, and the bouquet flew into the air. Philippe heard a shout, steps on the gravel, a voice he recognized that was choked with anger:

"If I ever get my hands on the idiot who did that...."

Feeling insulted, he renounced all idea of fleeing, and the Lady in White, irritated, found him by the gate. Her expression changed when she saw him, she unknitted her brows, shrugged her shoulders:

"I should've known," she said. "That wasn't very smart."

She was waiting for an excuse that wasn't forthcoming, since Phil, busy looking at her, mumbled to himself a thanks to her for dressing in white once more, and for her face discreetly highlighted with lipstick, and the sepia halos over her eyes. She brought a hand up to her cheek:

"Look, I'm bleeding!"

"Me, too," said Philippe stiffly.

And he held out his wounded hands. She leaned forward and squished under her finger a little pearl of blood on Phil's palm.

"Did you pick them for me?" she asked nonchalantly.

He only shook his head, chastising himself for displaying such boorish manners before an amiable and genteel woman. But she seemed neither angry nor surprised.

"You want to come in for a minute?"

He answered the same way, and his mute protest caused his hair to fly around his face, more handsome because of its strange severity, lacking in any other expression.

"What a blue these flowers are...it's indescribable...I'll plant them in my copper fire-basket...."

Phil's face relaxed a bit:

"I thought so," he said. "Or maybe in a gray stoneware pot."

"O.K., if that's what you'd like...a gray stoneware pot."

A sort of docility in Madame Dalleray's voice amazed Philippe. She became aware of it, looked him in the eye, regained her easy and almost masculine smile, and changed her tone of voice:

"Tell me, Monsieur Phil.... One question...a simple

question…this beautiful bouquet of sea holly, did you pick them for me, to please me?"

"Yes."

"Charming. To please me. But were you thinking more about my pleasure in receiving them, or about *your* pleasure in gathering and giving them to me?"

He could barely hear her, and looked at her as she spoke the way a deaf-mute would, his mind fixated on the shape of her mouth and the batting of her eyelashes. He didn't understand, and answered randomly:

"I thought you would enjoy them…and you gave me that orangeade…."

She pulled back the hand she had rested on Phil's arm, and swung open again the half-closed gate.

"All well and good, my little one. Now you have to go away and never come back."

"What?"

"No one asked you to be so obliging. You are now free of the kind concern that brought you here today and made you bombard me with sea holly. Farewell, Monsieur Phil. Unless…"

She pressed her bold forehead against the gate that she had quickly shut between them and looked Philippe up and down as he stood frozen on the little road.

"Unless one day I find you again right here, when you've

come back not to repay me for my orangeade with a thorny bouquet, but for some other reason...."

"Some other reason...."

"Your voice sounds so much like mine, Monsieur Phil! Then we'll see whose consent is up for grabs—yours or mine. I only like beggars and the hungry, Monsieur Phil. If you come back, come back with your hand outstretched.... Get going now, Monsieur Phil!"

She withdrew from the gate, and Philippe left. Chased away, even banished, he took with him only a man's pride, and in his memory the black arabesques of the gate were like a viburnum branch, crowning a feminine face, tattooed on the cheek with the sign of fresh blood.

"You're going to trip, Vinca, your shoe's untied. Wait a second."

Phil dropped down quickly, seized the two white wool ribbons and crossed them over a brown ankle, quivering, dry, the leg of a fine animal, made for running and jumping. Even the hardened epidermis, the numerous scars could not mask its gracefulness. Almost without flesh on the slight bone structure, just enough muscle to provide some curvature; Vinca's leg did not arouse desire, but the type of exaltation that a pure style evokes.

"Wait, I said! I can't tie your laces while you're walking!"

"Leave it alone."

Her naked foot, with only a canvas shoe, slipped between the hand that held it and jumped, as if it were flying away, over Phil's head as he knelt. He caught a whiff of lavender, ironed linen, and seaweed that made up Vinca's scent, and saw her three steps away from him. She examined him from head to toe and poured over him the dark and clouded light of her eyes, whose blue refused to imitate the sea's shifting nuances.

"What's come over you? This is really strange behavior! Excuse me, but don't I know how to tie a sandal? Trust me, Vinca, you're becoming impossible!"

Phil's chivalrous pose did not go well with his face of an offended Roman god, golden, crowned with black hair, his charm hardly threatened by the shadow of his future mustache—thick bristles tomorrow, downy velvet today.

Vinca did not come back. She seemed astonished and breathless as if Phil had chased after her.

"What's the matter? Did I hurt you? Did you get pricked by a thorn?"

She shook her head No, softened, sat down abruptly among the sage and the pink knotweeds, tugged the hem of her dress down to her ankles. An angular and pleasing quickness governed all her movements—an equilibrium as exceptional as a gift for choreography. Her tender and exclusive camaraderie for Phil had shaped her during their boyish games. They maintained a sporting rivalry that did not yield even to a love that was born with her. Despite the power that each day accrued monstrously, that little by little fed off of their trust, their sweetness, despite the love that changed the nature of their tenderness the way the colored water that roses drink changes their color, they sometimes forgot about their love.

Philippe could not stand Vinca's gaze for long, though its darkened azure was not in the least reproachful. She only seemed surprised, and breathed quickly, like a doe encountered during a stroll in the forest, a doe that stands suspended, stirred, instead of leaping away. She questioned her own instincts, rather than those of the kneeling boy whose touch she had fled; she knew she had just given in to her own defiance, a sort of revulsion, not modesty. There was no question of modesty alongside such a great love.

In a sudden warning, Vinca's vigilant purity perceived a feminine presence around Philippe. It happened that she was sniffing the air around him as if he had secretly been smoking, or had eaten a special treat. She interrupted their small talk with a silence as imperious as a leap, with a glance whose shock and weight he could sense. She freed her hand from its counterpart, smaller but less fine than hers, where her hand rested when they took a walk before dinner.

His third, his fourth visit to Madame Dalleray's, Phil had hid from Vinca without difficulty. But what good are distance and walls against the invisible antennae of a soul smitten with love when its antennae unfold, grope, uncover the blemish, and retract? Grafted onto their great secret, this little parasitic secret marked Philippe, who was in fact innocent, with a moral deformity. Vinca now found him soft when, confident in his despotism as a fraternal lover, he should have treated her like a slave. A bit of the affability of the unfaithful spouse slid into him and made her question him.

Having reprimanded Vinca for her strange mood, Philippe stuck to his superior attitude this time and took the road to the villa, keeping himself from running. Would he eat his afternoon snack one hour from now at Ker-Anna, as Madame Dalleray had begged him to do? Begged? She only knew how to give orders, and commanded with a disguised severity the boy she had raised to the rank of a starving beggar. A beggar in rebellion against humility who might, when he was far from her, think without gratitude of the woman who poured the cool drinks, the woman who peeled the fruit and whose white hands served and took care of the little, well-built novice who had dropped by. But how could this adolescent be called a novice, when love, since his childhood, had sanctified him as a man and kept him pure? Where she might have found a willing victim, enchanted to submit, Madame Dalleray encountered a dazzled and wary opponent. With his thirsty mouth and his outstretched hands, this beggar did not have the look of someone conquered.

He will defend himself, she conjectured. *He's holding back....* She was not yet ready to say, She's *holding him back.*

Philippe managed to yell in the direction of the house, to Vinca who remained in the sandy meadow:

"I'm going to get the second post. You need anything?"

A shake of her head turned Vinca's even hair into a sunlit wheel. Philippe jumped onto his bicycle.

Madame Dalleray did not *appear* to be expecting him—she was reading. But he was tipped off by the calculated shadows of the living room, the almost invisible table bearing the aromas of a late peach, red melons from Cyprus cut into crescent moons, and black coffee poured onto crushed ice.

Madame Dalleray put down her book and held out her hand to him without getting up. In the shadows he saw her white dress, white hand: her jet eyes, isolated below their sepia halos, moved with unaccustomed slowness.

"I hope I didn't wake you," said Phil, forcing himself to act with worldly politeness.

"No, certainly not. Is it hot? Are you hungry?"

"I don't know...."

He sighed, sincerely undecided. Since entering Ker-Anna he had been seized with a sort of thirst and with a sensitivity to edible odors which would have resembled an appetite if a nameless anxiety hadn't tightened his throat at the same time. But his hostess served him and he inhaled, on a little silver scoop, the red flesh of a melon powdered with sugar, impregnated with a trace of licorice alcohol.

"Your parents are well, Monsieur Phil?"

He looked at her, surprised. She seemed distracted and appeared not to have heard her own voice. His shirt cuff caught a spoon and it fell, ringing feebly as it hit the rug.

"Clumsy... Wait a second..."

With one hand she grabbed his fist, and with the other hand she rolled Phil's sleeve up to the elbow and firmly held the naked arm in her warm hand.

"Let me go!" shouted Phil.

He yanked his hand away violently. A saucer broke at his feet. In the buzzing in his ears he heard the echo of Vinca's cry: "Let go!" and he looked at Madame Dalleray with his eyes full of wrath and questions. She hadn't budged and the hand he had pulled back lay open on his knees like the hollow of a conch. For a long time Philippe weighed the meaning of his inability to move. He lowered his head, saw pass before his eyes two or three incoherent, ineluctable images of flight, as one flies in a dream, or of falling, as one falls in diving, at the instant when the folds of the wave are going to join with the face heading toward them—then, without rushing, with a reflective slowness, with a calculated courage, he placed his naked arm back in the open hand.

GREEN WHEAT

When Philippe left the house of the Lady in White it might have been one-thirty in the morning.

He had lain in wait for all the sounds and lights to die down before leaving his family's villa. A glass door, closed with a latch, then a wooden barrier shut with its own weight—beyond that, the road, freedom...Freedom? He had walked toward Ker-Anna hobbled by obstacles, sometimes stopping to catch his breath, his left hand resting on his heart, his head lowered, then raised like a dog barking at the moon. At the highest point on the coast, he had turned around to pick out in the midst of the cliffs the place where his parents were sleeping, and Vinca's parents—and Vinca. The third window, the little wooden balcony...she must be sleeping behind that pair of closed shutters. She had to be sleeping, turned a little on her side, her head on her arm, like a child hiding her face to cry, her even hair spread like a fan from her nape to her cheek. He had seen her asleep so many times since their childhood. He knew the melancholy and sweet position that she assumed only in her sleep.

The fear of telepathically awakening her soon turned Philippe back to the road, white in the milky night of the waxing moon that guided his steps. Worry, love, barely less powerful in the depths of an adolescent's sleep, he had felt them, vigilant, latching onto him. Could their weight, much more than the chilling fear that freezes a boy of sixteen on the road to his first fling, could their weight perhaps transform this test into drudgery, and delirious pride into curiosity without courage? But he had hesitated just a moment before speeding up along his route, with the same gesture of suffocation and calling out to the moon, on the other slope of the coast that he was climbing, on the way back, more slowly.

Two A.M., Philippe counted, his ear cocked toward the village clock. The four crystalline quarter-hours, the two grave hours traveled softly through the warm, salty fog. He automatically added, *The wind is shifting, I can hear the church clock—a change in the weather...* and the sound of this familiar phrase came to him from faraway, from a life that had elapsed. He sat down on the grassy edge of a flower bed in front of the villa and suddenly started to cry, and was ashamed of his tears, until he realized he was crying with pleasure.

Someone next to him let out a long sigh; at his feet the watchman's dog, hard to make out, was dozing on the sandy path. Phil leaned over, caressed its wild-boar hair, the dry nose of this friendly animal that had not barked.

"Fanfare...good old Fanfare...."

But the aging dog, with its personality so typical for Brittany, got up and went to lie back down a safe distance away, rustling like an old sack.

GREEN WHEAT

The neap tide, sleeping under the mist at the end of the meadow, sent toward the beach a little, weakened wave. From time to time the wave snapped feebly like wet linen. No bird was keeping vigil except for a sparrow-owl that was mockingly imitating the cat, sometimes from the top of an aspen whiter than the mist, sometimes from the row of spindle-trees.

Slowly, Philippe's thoughts began to assimilate the familiar and unrecognizable surroundings. This nocturnal peace that dispossesses man, offered him refuge, the necessary transition between his former life, the sweet country of all the summers he had spent and the place, the climate, where an indiscernible storm of colors, aromas, and lights were wheeling, their hidden source conveying a sharp sting or a pale and constrained layer.... Furniture and flowers seemed to lose their balance, the furniture with its skinny legs of a doe, the flowers revealing the plush underside of their leaves, their rigid stems in pure water. Such a treacherous place and climate where a hand, a woman's mouth could unleash at will the force that annihilates a tranquil universe, the cataclysm that had blessed—like the luminous bridge that rises in the heavens after lightning—the arc of a naked arm.

At least he had now left it behind him, this torment that he had just crossed through. He brought back with him only a swimmer's exhaustion, the vague and universal indulgence of a shipwrecked passenger setting foot on land. Luckier than other young men who—often tearing themselves to shreds in the process—end up exchanging a long period of anxiousness, fertile with unlimited daydreams for a pleasure that from now on will limit their dreams, he came back, heavy only with the usual stupor, conscious as the glutted drunk who feels the rocking, when he moves, of the cooled mass of wine from which the burning and airy force has escaped.

Day was still far off, but already half the night shone brighter than the other and divided the sky. A very small animal, a hedgehog or a rat, scraped the earth as it trotted along. The first breath of wind, forerunner of the dawn, rolled a few petals down the path, left them, vanished, and once again everything settled into stillness. Three bells peeled dreamily on a faraway clock, the first limpid and close by, two others muffled by a gust of wind. A couple of curlews passed over Philippe's head, low enough for him to hear the cry of their outspread wings flapping over the water, and their whimpering in this adolescent's open and defenseless memory dove to the depths of fifteen pure years, years that were clinging to a blonde shore, to a child who was growing up by his side, holding up her blonde and upright head like a stalk of wheat.

He got up, making a physical effort to recognize himself, to insist that the boy who had just rested there—next to the white fence, next to the sleeping dog—was the same one who, the night before, had turned fearfully toward Ker-Anna leaning against the white fence, distractedly caressing the sleeping dog. But he couldn't.

He stroked his face with his two warm hands. They seemed softer than normal, impregnated with a perfume that fled when his nostrils tried to memorize it, but which vibrated around him, like the aroma of certain odiferous plants with their fragile foliage. At that moment, the glow of a lamp switched on between the slats of the shutters and switched off soon afterward, in Vinca's room.

She's not asleep. She just checked what time it is. Why isn't she sleeping?

Through the walls, he knew just how, with her arm extended, Vinca had switched on the lamp, glanced at the watch hanging on the brass bed, then had thrown her head back against the pillow, turning off the lamp, her head and hair smelling like a coddled child and lavender. He knew that because of the sultry night a browned shoulder, with a strap of white skin where her bathing suit kept the sun off her, remained naked, and the shape of his friend's long and vigorous body—familiar body, endowed each year with new and anticipated beauty—appeared before him, knocking him almost senseless.

This body—with the use love could make of it, with its inevitable purposes—what could this body have in common with another woman's, devoted to delicate abductions, gifted with a genius for despoiling, with a passionate implacability, the body of an enchantress and her hypocritical curriculum?

"Never!" he said out loud.

Yesterday, with a patient heart, he was still measuring the

time until Vinca would belong to him. Today, paled by lessons that left his body trembling with the sweetness of defeat, Philippe recoiled with all of his being before an insane image.

"Never!"

Dawn came quickly. But no wind chased away the salty mist where the red of the rising daybreak advanced layer by layer. Philippe crossed the villa's threshold, walked silently upstairs toward his room still full of the stifling night, and flung open the shutters, in a hurry to confront in a mirror his new face, the face of a man.

He saw, in a face thinned by weariness, languid eyes, enlarged by the circles under them, a mouth that had touched lipstick and remained a bit made-up, black hair mussed over his brow— plaintive traits, resembling less a man than a bruised girl.

By the time Philippe was falling asleep, the goldfinches were already clamoring for the seeds that Vinca threw them by the fistful in the morning. Philippe's throbbing sleep suffered from their soft cries, and his half-dream shed them in curled metal shavings, torn from the painful cap that covered his skull. Too beautiful, the day resounded with laying hens, bees, wheat threshers as he woke up completely; the sea was turning green, brushed back by the fresh nor'wester, and Vinca laughed, dressed all in white, under the window.

"What's the matter with him? What is the matter? Hey, Phil! Have you got sleeping sickness?"

And the familiar Shadows, who had become almost invisible, like an old stain on a wall, like ivy or lichen, the Shadows whom the adolescents held in disdain, repeated all around her:

"What's the matter with him? What is the matter? He must be eating poppies!"

From upstairs he looked out the window at them. His mouth was half-open, with a sort of ingenuous horror on his face, and he was so pale that Vinca's laugh died down, extinguishing the general laughter:

"Oh! Are you sick?"

He recoiled as if Vinca had hurled a stone at him.

"Sick? I'll show you if I'm sick! First of all, what time is it?"

The laughter started up again down below:

"A quarter to eleven, sleepyhead! Let's go swimming!"

He nodded yes, closed the window, and the panes draped in tulle drove him back toward that nocturnal abyss where the eddy of a memory stretched its limbs, black, unctuous, unwinding slowly between pulsing flashes that were hoisting themselves up into the light of day, taking on the color of gold, of flesh, of the glitter of a moist eye, of a ring or a fingernail. . . .

He threw off his pajamas, quickly pulled on his bathing suit, and instead of going downstairs half-naked, as he did every day, he carefully knotted the belt of his robe.

Colette

Vinca was waiting for him in the meadow by the sea, and was peacefully toasting in the sun her long legs, her slender arms as brown as country bread. The incomparable blue of her eyes, under the faded blue scarf, filled Philippe with a thirst for fresh water, with a desire for salty billows and a stiff wind. At the same time, he contemplated the obvious power of a body that each day became more feminine, the hard knees delicately chiseled, the long thigh muscles, and the proud, arched torso.

She's so solid! he thought, with a sort of fear.

They dove together, and while Vinca joyously battered the weak waves with her arms and legs, spitting out water as she sang, Philippe, pale, struggled not to tremble and swam with his teeth clenched. When Vinca's naked feet squeezed one of his feet, Phil suddenly stopped swimming, slid straight down, and reappeared several seconds later. But he didn't retaliate, and avoided their usual daily shouting, and the sea-lion jousts and combat that made their swim the best hour of the day.

The hot sand gathered them in, and they rubbed themselves dry vigorously and thoroughly. Vinca, armed with a pebble, took aim at a horned reef, hit it from a distance of fifty meters, and Philippe defiantly marveled at her, forgetting that he himself had taught his girlfriend these boyish games. He felt soft, superior to himself, almost faint, and no masculine arrogance revealed that he had fled the home of his youth the night before to run off to his first amorous adventure.

"Noon, Phil! The church bells are ringing noon. You hear them?"

Standing up, Vinca shook out her wet and even hair. Her first steps toward the villa crushed a little crab that cracked like a nut, and Philippe winced painfully.

"What is it?" said Vinca.

"You crushed that little crab."

She turned around, the bright sun catching the sunburnt peaches of her cheeks, her eyes so unquestionably blue, her white teeth, and the red interior of her mouth.

"So what? Is that the first time? What about when you bait the net with a cut-up crab?"

She ran ahead of Philippe and with one leap jumped over a hollow in the dunes. For a fraction of a second he glimpsed her suspended, detached from the ground, her feet together, leaning forward with her arms rounded as if she were gathering up an armful of air.

And I thought she was sweet, Philippe brooded.

Lunch prevented him from reaching into his nocturnal memories again, drowsy in the middle of the day, and barely stirring in their black quarters. He suffered as they complimented his poetic pallor, criticized his silence and lack of appetite. Vinca devoured everything and shone with a cheerfulness that pained him. Phil observed her without benevolence, noticed how vigorously her hands crushed the lobster, the haughty toss of her neck as it shook back her hair.

I should be glad, he thought. *She doesn't suspect a thing.* But at the same time that inexorable calm hurt him, and at heart what he needed was for Vinca to tremble like grass, to be disheartened by a betrayal that she should have detected wandering off course like one of those hesitant storms that whirl in summer around the bays of Brittany.

She says she loves me. She does love me. But she was more worried before. . . .

After lunch, Vinca danced to phonograph records with Lisette. She insisted that Philippe dance, too. She checked the tidal almanac, readied the nets for the four o'clock low tides, filled Philippe and the villa with the shouts of a high school student, with requests for tarred string, for the old fishing knife, spreading in her wake the odor of her tattered fishing sweater, which smelled of iodine and seaweed. Philippe, weary, finally invaded by the sleepiness that follows catastrophes and great happiness, followed her with a vindictive look and nervously clenched his fists.

With three words I could shut her up! But he knew he would not utter those three words, and he was yearning to sleep in a hollow in the hot dunes, his head in Vinca's lap. . . .

All along the shoreline they found shrimp, and gurnards inflating to scare off predators, with their fins like fans, and their rainbow throats. But Phil halfheartedly pursued the small fry of the rocks and waves. He could barely stand the reflection of the sun in the tide pools and slipped like a novice on the wrack-grass's slick hair. He captured a lobster and Vinca poked mercilessly at the "dock"—a conger-eel's dwelling.

"You can see he's in there!" she shouted, showing him the end of the iron hook, tinted with pink blood.

Philippe turned pale and shut his eyes.

"Leave the poor thing alone." He choked on the words.

"You're kidding! I guarantee you I'm going to get it.... What's the matter with you?"

"Nothing."

He was hiding, as best he could, a pain he didn't understand. What had he won the night before in the perfumed shadows, between jealous arms, that made him a man and victorious? The right to suffer? The right to faint with weakness in front of a hard and innocent child? The right to tremble inexplicably, faced with the delicate life of animals and the sight of blood?

Suffocating, he took a deep breath, brought his hands up to his face and burst into sobs. He cried so violently that he had to sit down, and Vinca remained standing, armed with her hook soaked in blood, like a torturer. She leaned over him, asked no questions, but listened like a musician to the pitches, the new and intelligible modulation of his sobs. She stretched out her hand toward Philippe's forehead, and pulled it back before making contact. Stupor left her face and was replaced by a severe expression, a bitter and sad grimace that was ageless, a contempt, completely virile, for the suspicious weakness of this boy in tears. Then she carefully collected her raffia basket that the fish were jumping in, and her net, and tucking her iron hook into her belt like a sword, she walked away with a determined gait, and did not look back.

He didn't see her again until just before dinner. She had changed out of her fishing outfit into a blue crepe dress, faithful to the color of her eyes. It was scalloped in pink. He noticed she had on white stockings and buckskin shoes, and this Sunday attire worried him.

"Are we having company for dinner?" he asked one of the family Shadows.

"Count the place settings," answered the Shadow with a shrug of the shoulders.

August was ending, and they were already dining by the glow of lamplight, the open doors greeting the green sunset, where a thin spindle of pink copper still floated. The empty sea, blue-black as a swallow's feathers, was sleeping, and when the dinner table conversation fell silent, they could hear the tired, calm, and regular rise of the neap tide. Philippe sought out Vinca's gaze between the Shadows, to test the power of that invisible thread that had linked them for so many years and had preserved them, exalted and pure, from the melancholy that descended over the ends of meals, the ends of seasons, the ends of days. But she stared down at her plate, and the light from the hanging lamp polished her curved eyelids, her round and browned cheeks, her little chin. He felt abandoned, and he searched—beyond the lion-shaped peninsula jutting out, crowned by three stars over the sea—for the road, white in the night, that led to Ker-Anna. A few hours more, a bit more blue ash in that sky tinged as if by dawn, a few more ritual phrases: "Look at that, already ten o'clock. Children, you don't look like you believe that we go to bed at ten o'clock around here." "Well, I didn't do anything earth-shattering today, Madame Audebert, but I'm as tired as if I'd been going non-stop...." A few more dishes tinkling in the sink, the rough splashing of dominoes on the naked table, one more moan of protest from Lisette who, three quarters asleep, refused to go to bed. One more attempt to win back Vinca's glance, her inner smile, her trust, mysteriously wounded, and the hour would chime, the same hour when Philippe, the night before, had slipped furtively away. He thought about it with no precise desire in mind, without a plan, and as if forced by Vinca's mood to beat a retreat to another refuge, another soothing shoulder, an efficient warmth, urgently needed by this convalescent of pleasure, not to mention how bruised he felt by the passionate hostility of that adolescent girl.

The rites were performed one after another; the maid carried off a whining Lisette, and Madame Ferret slapped the double six down onto the mirrored table.

"Do you want to come outside, Vinca? It's annoying how these silkworm moths smash into all the lamps. . . ."

She followed him without answering and they found again, near the sea, the light that lingers after dusk.

"You don't want me to go get your scarf?"

"No, thanks."

They walked together, bathed in that blue vapor that rose from the meadow by the sea, smelling of wild thyme. Philippe refrained from taking his friend's arm, and his discretion terrified him.

My God, what's happened between us? Have we lost one another? Since she doesn't know what happened back there, maybe all I have to do is forget about it, and we'll be happy in the same way we were before, unhappy in the same way we were before, united just as before?

But he couldn't place his blind faith in this wish, since Vinca was walking by his side, cold and mild as if her great love had left her, and she didn't sense her companion's anxiousness. And then Phil felt *that hour* approaching and suffered a trepidation equal to the fever that he'd had the day after he had been pricked by a sting-fish, when he felt the rising tide reawaken a burning in his bandaged arm.

He stopped, wiped his brow:

"It's like I'm choking. I don't feel well, Vinca."

"No, not well," echoed Vinca's voice.

He believed they had made a truce, and he quickly answered using both his voice and gestures:

"Oh, you're so sweet! Oh, my darling!"

"No," interrupted the other voice, "I'm not sweet."

This childlike sentence left Philippe still hoping, and he seized his friend's bare arm.

"You're angry, I know, that I cried today like a woman."

"No, not like a woman."

He blushed in the shadows, and tried to explain himself:

"You understand, it was about that eel you were torturing in his hole...that animal's blood on your lobster hook. I suddenly just felt heartsick...."

"Yeah, right, your heart...it felt sick...."

Her voice sounded so knowing that Philippe was scared to breathe. *She's figured it all out.* He was waiting for her crushing pronouncement, an explosion of tears, complaints. But Vinca remained mute, and after a long while, like the calm that follows lightning, he risked a timid question:

"And just that weakness is enough to make you act as if you don't love me any more?"

Vinca turned toward him the bright and nebulous spot of her face, pressed between the two rigid rows of her hair:

"Phil, I do still love you. Unfortunately, this doesn't change a thing."

He felt his leaping heart smash against his chest:

75

"It doesn't? So you'll forgive me for acting like a little girl, so ridiculous?"

She only hesitated a second:

"Of course I'm going to forgive you, Phil. But even that won't change a thing."

"About what?"

"About us, Phil."

She spoke with a sibylline softness that he didn't dare challenge further, and in which he didn't dare rejoice. Vinca no doubt followed the steps of his mental twists and turns, since she subtly added:

"Do you remember the scenes you made, and the ones I made—it wasn't even three weeks ago—when we were so upset at having to cool off for four or five years before getting married? My poor Phil, I really wish I could turn the clock back and be a child again today."

He waited for her to underline, to comment on that skillful, that insidious "today," hanging in front of him in the pure and blue air of that August night. But Vinca already knew how to arm herself with silence. He insisted:

"So, you're not holding it against me? Tomorrow we'll be... we'll be Vinca and Phil, the way we always were? Forever?"

"Forever—if you want it, Phil... C'mon, let's go back inside. It's cold out here."

She hadn't repeated, "the way we always were." But he contented himself with this incomplete vow and with the small, cold hand he held for a moment in his own. At that instant the clanging of the well-chain, the empty bucket bonging against the lip of the well, the curtains in an open window straining till the rod creaked, the last human sounds of the day rang for Philippe the hour, the same hour he had lain in wait for the night before, to open the villa door again and secretly run out...the muted, red light of an unfamiliar room...the black joy, death bit by bit, life regained through the slow beating of a wing.

As if he had been waiting since the night before for a sort of absolution from Vinca, an ambiguous absolution that she had just granted him with such sincerity in her voice, with so much reticence in her words, he suddenly could measure, as a man, the gift that a beautiful, commanding she-devil had given to him.

"Have you set the date when you're leaving for Paris?" asked Madame Dalleray.

"We're still planning to be back September twenty-fifth," Philippe answered. "Sometimes, depending on when Sunday falls in the month, we leave on the twenty-third or the twenty-fourth, or even the twenty-sixth. But it hardly ever varies more than two days."

"I see. The long and the short of it is, you're leaving in two weeks. Two weeks from now, at this time...."

Philippe tore his eyes away from the sea, flat and white near the sand—under the low clouds in the distance its color was the back of a tuna—and he turned with astonishment toward Madame Dalleray. Wrapped in an ample white cloth like the dresses of Tahitian women, she smoked sternly, her hair cut crisply, her face powdered with a powder that matched her skin, and nothing in her revealed that this young man seated not far from her, handsome and tan as she herself was, meant anything more to her than a younger brother.

"So, two weeks from now, at this time of day, you'll be— where?"

"I'll be...in the Bois, on the lake. Or at the Boulogne tennis courts, with...with friends."

He blushed, since he had barely caught Vinca's name before it slipped out of his lips, and Madame Dalleray smiled that virile smile that often made her look like a handsome boy. Philippe turned back toward the sea to hide at least his face, which betrayed the spiteful attitude of an angry little god. A firm and velvety hand rested on his own. Then, with his glance fixed on the tarnished sea, an expression of blessèd agony rose from his slack mouth, migrated up to his eyes, where a black and white spark shot out from between his lids.

"Don't be sad," said Madame Dalleray, softly.

"I'm not sad," Philippe protested vigorously. "You wouldn't understand...."

Her head, with its lustrous hair, tilted to one side.

"That's true. I couldn't understand. Not everything."

"Oh. . . ."

With a zealot's defiance Philippe contemplated the woman who had freed him from an awful secret. Did a soft cry, muffled like the scream of someone having his throat cut, still resound in her little, reddish ears? Those arms, rich with muscles he could barely see, had carried him, light, swooning, out of this world; her mouth, stingy with words, had leaned over and whispered to him one single, all-powerful word and murmured, indistinctly, a song that came like a hushed echo from the depths where life is a mere trembling. . . . She knew everything.

"Not everything," she repeated, as if Philippe's silence had sought a response. "But you don't like me to ask questions. And sometimes I'm a bit indiscreet."

Yes, like lightning, thought Philippe. *Just a zigzag of light and you give up to her what even broad daylight left in shadow.*

"I merely wanted to know if you'll be glad when you leave me."

The young man looked down at his bare feet. A loose garment of embroidered silk disguised him as an oriental pasha, embellished his good looks.

"How about you?" he asked clumsily.

The ash of the cigarette Madame Dalleray was holding between her fingers dropped onto the rug.

"This is not about me. This concerns Philippe Audebert and not Camille Dalleray."

79

He raised his eyes, astonished again by her asexual name. *Camille... It's true, her name is Camille. She doesn't really need it. I always think of her as Madame Dalleray, the Lady in White, or She...*

She smoked slowly, contemplating the sea. Young? Definitely young, between thirty and thirty-two. Impenetrable as calm beings are, whose expression never goes beyond restrained irony, a smile, and seriousness. Without once looking away from the expanse where the storm was brewing, she placed her hand again on Philippe's and pressed it, indifferent to him in her solitary, egotistical pleasure. Under this little, powerful hand, he spoke, awkward about pouring out his confession, as a squeezed fruit spills out its nectar:

"Sure I'll be sad. But I hope I won't be unhappy."

"Oh? And why do you hope that?"

He smiled at her weakly. He was touching, clumsy—what she secretly loved him to be.

"Because," he answered, "I think you'll come up with some way.... Will you come up with some way?"

She shrugged her shoulders, raised her Persian eyebrows. She had to push herself a bit to endow her smile with its usual serenity and disdain.

"Some way..." she repeated, "you mean, if I interpret you correctly, that I will invite you to my house, as I do here, if I still choose to, and the only thing you will have to worry about is

meeting me, when you've fulfilled your obligations for school
and . . . to your family, shall we say?"

He appeared surprised by her tone of voice, but did not
shirk Madame Dalleray's glance:

"Yes," he answered. "What else am I supposed to do? You
blame me for that? I'm not some little street urchin who can do
whatever he wants. And I'm only sixteen and a half!"

The blood slowly rose to her cheeks.

"I'm not blaming you for anything. But doesn't it occur to
you that a woman . . . some other woman, naturally, might be
shocked to realize that what you want is just an hour alone with
her—that's all, nothing more?"

Philippe listened to her with a schoolboy's loyal attention, his
eyes wide open, fixed on that reticent mouth, on those jealous
eyes that, nevertheless, asked for nothing.

"No," he said without hesitation. "I can't imagine that you'd
be hurt by that. 'That's all?' Oh . . . *that's* all. . . ."

He fell silent, nonplussed again by the same paleness, the same
blissful dismay, and Camille Dalleray's calm boldness wavered,
weighing how much respect she owed to this work she had created.
As if dazzled, Philippe let his head fall forward, and this gesture of
submission intoxicated his conqueror for a moment.

"You love me?" she asked in a quiet voice.

He shuddered, looked at her, scared.

"Why...why are you asking me?"

She regained her composure, her doubting smile.

"Just for fun, Philippe."

His eyes continued to question her, while they blamed her for speaking so recklessly.

A grown man would just have said "yes," she thought. But this child, if I insist on it, will cry and shout at me through his tears, his kisses, that he doesn't love me. Am I going to insist? Then I'd have to pursue him, or even listen to him as he trembles, and learn from his lips the exact extent of my advantage.

She experienced a slight and painful contraction of her heart and stood up nonchalantly to walk over toward the view of the bay, as if she had forgotten Phil's presence. The smell of little blue mussels, uncovered four hours earlier at the foot of the rocks and discolored by the sea water, wafted in along with the thick, boiled, elder tree bark aroma that privet emits as its blooms start to wilt.

Leaning on her elbows, distracted, Madame Dalleray felt the presence of the young man stretched out behind her, the weight of a desire that would not leave her.

He's waiting for me, calculating the pleasure he can expect. What I got out of him was within the reach of any other woman who might have encountered him. But this shopkeeper's son turns up his nose if I ask him for news about his family, puts on airs when he talks to me about his high school, and locks himself in a fortress of silence and modesty when he hears the name Vinca.... He only learned from me what was easiest....Easiest.... Each time he comes here he brings with him, sets down, and picks up at the same time as his clothes, his...

She realized she had hesitated before the word "love," and she moved away from the window. Philippe eagerly followed her approach. She put her arms around his shoulders, and with a slightly brutal push she made his brown head capsize onto her bare arm. With this burden, she rushed toward the narrow and dark kingdom where her pride could believe that a moan is a confession of distress, and where the aggressive beggars of her sort drink the illusion of generosity.

A light rain, lasting a few hours of the night, had sprayed the sage, varnished the privet, the motionless leaves of the magnolia. Without crushing it, the rain had studded with pearls the protective gauze that enveloped the nest of processionary caterpillars in a pine tree. The wind left the sea in peace, but sung under the doors in a weak and tempting voice, heavy with memories of the year gone by, spoke in muffled whispers of roasted chestnuts and ripe apples.... Incited by the wind, Philippe got dressed on waking in a dark blue sweater he put on under a cloth jacket, was the last to eat breakfast, as often happened now that his sleep, less pure and tranquil, began so late at night. He ran, hunting for Vinca, as if he had stepped beyond the shadow of a wall and was searching for a sunlit green. But he didn't find her either in the hallway, where the humidity brought back to life the smell of varnished woodwork and hemp cloth, or on the lawn. Impalpable rain fumed into the air like incense and stuck to the skin without moistening it. An aspen leaf, yellow, detached, hovered in the air a second in front of Philippe with intentional grace, then flipped over and plummeted, suddenly possessing invisible weight. He cocked his ears, heard in the kitchen the hibernal sound of coal being poured into the stove. In a bedroom, little Lisette protested sharply, then cried for a moment.

"Lisette!" called Philippe. "Lisette, where's your sister?"

"I don't know!" groaned a little voice congested with tears.

A sudden squall of wind plucked a tile from the roof and dashed it to pieces at Philippe's feet, and he looked at it as stupefied as if fate had broken a mirror in front of him that promised seven years of bad luck. He felt like a little boy, exiled from happiness. He had no desire to call out to the woman who, in the villa shaded with pines, there on the other side of the lion-shaped cape, would have loved to see him pusillanimous and leaning toward the pull of her indomitable feminine energy. He searched all over the house, found neither his friend's blonde head, nor her blue dress as blue as sea holly, nor her white terry-cloth dress, white as a fresh mushroom. Two long brown legs, with their lean and fine knees, weren't rushing to meet him; two blue eyes, lavished with two or three blues and a touch of mauve, didn't sprout up anywhere to quench his own.

"Vinca! Hey, where are you, Vinca?"

"Right over here," answered a calm voice, close by.

"In the shed?"

"In the shed."

Squatting down in the cold light of a windowless shelter that sunlight entered only through the door, she was shaking out fabrics spread out on an old sheet.

"What are you doing?"

"You can see for yourself. Arranging. Sorting. We're leaving soon, so I have to…Mama told me I had to…"

Vinca looked at Philippe and stopped work, hugging her drawn-up knees. She seemed humble and patient, and that annoyed him.

"What's the rush to do all that now? Why are you doing it yourself?"

"Who else will do it? If Mama starts to, she'll get rheumatism in her chest again."

"The maid can just as well…"

Vinca shrugged her shoulders and resumed her task, softly talking to herself, the way working women buzz in little modest voices:

"These are Lisette's swimsuits…the green one…the blue one…the striped…might as well throw them out, for all they're worth. This is my dress with the pink scallops…it might be worth another wash…. A pair, two pairs, three pairs of my espadrilles…. And these are Phil's…another one of Phil's….

Two old mesh shirts of Phil's . . . the sleeve holes are torn, but the fronts are fine. . . ."

She held up the perforated cloth, found two rips, pouted. Philippe contemplated her without gratitude, hurting and hostile. The morning hour hurt him, also the gray lighting under the tile roof, even her simple task. A comparison, not at all inspired by the hidden hours of love back in Ker-Anna, began here, a comparison that hadn't yet reached Vinca's body, Vinca— the religion of his whole childhood. Vinca respectfully abandoned for the sake of the dramatic and necessary intox- ication of his first fling.

A comparison began here, among these worn-out clothes, scattered over a mended sheet, between these unplastered brick walls, before this child in an off-violet smock with faded shoulders. On her knees, she interrupted her work to throw back her well-shaped hair, that her daily swim and the salt air maintained in a humid and soft state. Less cheerful for the last two weeks, she seemed calmer, and her moods had an obstinate evenness that worried Philippe. Had she really wanted to die with him, rather than wait for a time when they could love freely, this premature housewife with her Joan of Arc haircut? The boy with knitted brows measured the change in her, but he hardly thought about Vinca while he contemplated her. In her presence, the fear of losing her left him, and the urgent need to win her back no longer tormented him. But a comparison began, because of her.

His new ability to feel, to suffer unexpectedly, the intolerance that a beautiful pirate had recently endowed him with, were inflamed by the smallest shock, and so was his loyal injustice, his first pangs of superiority that consisted of reproaching mediocrity for its mediocrity and its philosophy. He discovered, not only the world of emotions that is cavalierly called physical, but also the need to materially beautify an altar where an insufficient perfection trembled. He experienced the birth of a hunger for what satisfied the hand, the ear, and the eye—velvet, the studied music of a voice, perfumes. He did not criticize himself for this, since he felt better when in contact with that inebriating excess; and certain vestments of oriental silk, donned in the shadows of Ker-Anna, ennobled his soul.

He obeyed, awkwardly, an imprecise and generous plan. Neglecting to reveal to himself that he hoped for a Vinca who was incomparable, bedecked, rubbed with balm, he limited himself to perceiving the sorrow he felt in seeing her prostrate, naively unattractive. A few harsh words escaped him—Vinca did not reply. He became bitter, and she answered only enough to make him resort to insults, then ashamed of his violence. He took a moment to get hold of himself, to make excuses with a sort of flat contrition that he found pleasant. Meanwhile Vinca, with her patient hands, linked the sandals, pair by pair, turned inside out the pockets of the worn jackets, full of pink shells and dried sea horses.

87

"Not only that, it's your fault," Philippe concluded. "You don't answer.... Then I get carried away, carried away.... You let yourself be mistreated. Why?"

She enveloped him in the look of a wise woman, ripened by the calculations and concessions of a great love:

"At least when you're tormenting me," she said, "I know that you're still here...."

It's ending between us, right here, this year, thought Philippe somberly, as he looked out over the sea. *Vinca and I, a being just double enough to be twice as happy as one alone, the being that was Phil-and-Vinca is going to die here, this year. It's horrible! Can't I do something to stop it? And I'm not doing a thing about it.... And tonight, after ten o'clock, maybe I'll go once more, for the last time this vacation, to Madame Dalleray's....*

He dropped his head. His black hair hung down, like dripping tears.

If I had to go now, at this moment, to Madame Dalleray's, I'd refuse. Why?

White under a mournful sun squeezed between two storm clouds, the road that led to Ker-Anna hugged the side of the hill, rose, then hid its destination beyond a bouquet of stiff juniper trees, gray with dust. Philippe averted his gaze, seized by a repugnance that didn't fool him in the least. *Yes, but tonight...*

After three afternoon snacks at Ker-Anna, he renounced his

diurnal visits, fearing his family might worry and Vinca would become suspicious. Besides, with his extreme youth he quickly grew tired of inventing alibis. He also mistrusted the strong and resinous perfume that permeated Ker-Anna and the body, naked or veiled, of the woman he named in a low voice, alternately with the pride of a boyish libertine and the melancholy remorse of a husband who has cheated on his dear wife, his mistress, and sometimes, his master.

Whether or not they find out, it has to end here. Why?

No book, among all the books he had freely read, elbows on the sand, or hidden in his room, more from modesty than from fear, had taught him that someone had to perish in such an ordinary shipwreck. Novels filled a hundred pages or more leading up to physical love, the act itself took fifteen lines, and Philippe ransacked his memory in vain for a book where a young man does not give up his childhood and chastity in a single fall, but staggers through jolts that are deep—almost seismic—and go on for days and days.

Philippe got up, walked along the meadow by the sea, nibbled and melted at the edges by the equinoctial tides. A gorse bush, blooming again, leaned toward the beach, held up and sustained by a scraggly head of roots. *When I was young,* Philippe said to himself, *that gorse bush didn't lean toward the beach. The sea has eaten all that up—at least a few feet of it—while I was growing up. . . . And Vinca insists it's the gorse bush that moved. . . .*

Not far from the gorse bush, a round valley was scooped out of the dunes, carpeted with sea holly. Because of the color of the flowers they called that valley "Vinca's Eyes." That was the spot where one day Phil had secretly gathered a bunch of holly in bloom, the thorny homage he tossed over the wall of Ker-Anna. Today the dry flowers, on the sides of the valley, seemed burnt. Philippe stopped there a moment, too young to smile at the mysterious meaning that love gave to dead flowers, to a wounded bird, to a cracked ring, and he shook off his pain, bucked up his shoulders, threw back his hair in a standard gesture of pride, inwardly reproaching himself like a character in an adventure novel for children just old enough for first communion.

I'm sick of this weakness! It's true. This year I can actually say to myself—I'm a man! And as for my future...

He heard himself thinking these thoughts and blushed. His future? A month ago he could still contemplate it. He saw, a month ago, his future painted with precise and puerile detail against a large, blurry background—the future with its entryway full of examinations, starting to work on his baccalaureate again, thankless work accepted without too much bitterness because, "we have to, don't we"—the future and Vinca, the former rich because of the latter, the future cursed or blessed in Vinca's name.

I was in such a hurry at the beginning of the vacation, Philippe mused. *But now....* A smile flitted across his lips, the look of an unhappy man. His lip was growing darker every day, the sprouting of the

first coat, downy and fine, which is to mustaches as hay in the
forest is to the stiff grass of the fields, and it made his mouth
swell a bit and inflamed it like the mouth of a melancholy child.
It was to this mouth that her glance was drawn and drawn again,
the impenetrable glance, almost vindictive, of Camille Dalleray.

*My future, let's see, my future . . . it's very simple . . . if I don't study law,
my future will be Papa's store, ice boxes for hotels, chateaux; headlights, spare
parts, and hardware for cars. My baccalaureate, and right after it the store,
clients, correspondence. . . . Papa doesn't earn enough there to get his own car. . . .
Oh, but there's my military service . . . what was I thinking of? . . . Then let's say
after my baccalaureate. . . .*

He stopped short, turned back by a limitless boredom, by a
profound indifference to all that this future without secrets con-
cealed. "If you end up doing your military service near Paris, then
during that time, I . . ." Vinca's quiet, loving voice murmured in
Philippe's memory twenty plans that dated from this very year, and
now lay flat and pale, cut out of paper printed only in a dull black.
The colorful zone of his hope did not go beyond that very day, the
dinner hour, to playing chess with Vinca or Lisette—better Lisette,
whose aggressive eight years, sharp eyes, and precocious calculations
lightened Philippe's emotional burden—in fact, the hour when he
would surrender to pleasure. *Still,* he thought, *I'm not sure yet I'll go. No.
I'm not like some madman, not counting the minutes, not turned toward Ker-Anna
like a sunflower toward the light, I certainly can still claim the right to be myself, to
keep moving forward, to take pleasure in everything I loved before. . . .*

He didn't realize that in using that word, he planted it solidly between the two parts of his existence. He didn't know yet for how long all the events of his life would have to stumble against that milestone, that miraculous and banal landmark: *Oh, yes, that was* before.... *I remember now, that happened a bit* afterward....

He thought with disdain and jealousy of his school friends, who trembled with anticipation on that unspeakable threshold that they passed through whistling to themselves, liars, braggarts, disgust sapping their color. Then they forgot about it, then they came back to it, all without interrupting their studies, their games, their clandestine cigars, and debates on politics and sports. *Me, on the other hand.... Then She's to blame. It's her fault I don't hope for anything, not even for her?*

A "cork" of fog, that had come in from the open sea, was approaching the coast. It had been nothing more than a little, unraveled curtain on the water, wandering, hardly capable of hiding a little rocky isle. A stream of wind had just grabbed hold of it, hauled it in, and dropped it dizzily on the bay, piled up, opaque. In one minute Philippe, drowning in fog, saw the sea disappear along with the beach and his house, and coughed through a steam bath. Used to the marvels of a marine climate, he waited for another arm of wind to scatter the first one, and grew accustomed to that limbo, to that symbolic blindness, in the depths of which a calm face was shining, flung out from its hair like a pure moon—and from its idle hands barely gesturing.

Green Wheat

She's unshakeable... but tell her to give me back the course of time, my hurry, my impatience, my curiosity.... It's not fair.... It's not fair.... She makes me so mad!

He tried out revolt and ingratitude. A child of sixteen and a half does not know that those whom love makes so impatient to live and die are waylaid by the beautiful missionaries of an impenetrable order, heavy with the weight of flesh that stops time and lulls the mind to sleep, contented, while tutoring the body to ripen in their shadow.

The cork of fog was suddenly pulled out, sucked into the air, like a sheet lifted off the meadow, leaving an ephemeral fringe of water on each blade of grass, pearls of dew on the plush leaves, a moist varnish on the glabrous leaves.

The September sun poured down a sharp, yellow light that rejuvenated on the sea, blue in the distance, tinted green at the edge by submerged sands.

After the sea mist had passed, Philippe, bathed in air and light, breathed with joy as if bursting out of a stifling passageway. He turned toward the land to see the streaming gold of the gorse blooming again in the fissures in the rocks, and was startled to find behind him, like a sprite carried in and forgotten by the mist, a silent little boy.

"What do you want, boy? Don't you work for that woman who sells fish in Cancale?"

"Yeah, that's me," said the boy.

"No one's home in the kitchen? Are you looking for someone?"

The little boy shook the dust off his reddish hair.

"The lady told me ..."

"What lady?"

"She said: 'Tell Monsieur Phil that I've left.'"

"What lady?"

"I don't know. She said, 'Tell Monsieur Phil that I had to leave today.'"

"Where did she tell you that? Along the road?"

"Yes ... from her car."

"From her car...."

Philippe closed his eyes for a second, ran his hand across his forehead, whistling softly for emphasis: "Shew...shew... Shew.... From her car...right. Shew...shew...." He opened his eyes again, looked around for the messenger, who was no longer there, and Philippe thought he must have had one of those quick dreams, roughly sketched, brutally erased, that sprung from afternoon naps. But he spied the maleficent child up on a path along the cliff. The boy was walking away, with his stubble of hair and a square, bluish patch on his shorts.

Philippe assumed a foolish and pompous pose as if the boy from Cancale could still see him.

Well ... that doesn't change much, her being gone. One day either way.... She had to leave eventually!

94

But a strange ache, almost entirely physical, was taking shape in him, near his stomach. He let the ache grow, tilting his head intelligently, as if he were listening to some mysterious advice.

Maybe with a bicycle.... But what if she's not alone? I should've asked the kid if she was alone....

Far away a car along the coast road blew its horn. The grave and sustained sound suspended for a moment the ache he felt, but it clobbered Philippe one moment later, like the cramp from a blow below the belt.

At least I won't have to wonder if I'm going to her house tonight....

Suddenly he imagined the Ker-Anna villa locked up under the moon, its gray shutters, its black iron gate, the geraniums held prisoner, and he shivered. He lay down in a fold of the dry meadow, rolled over on his back like a young hunting dog suffering from "the sickness," and he began to scrape the sandy grass over and over with his feet. He shut his eyes, since the racing of the huge clouds, that thick and swelling whiteness, filled him with a touch of nausea. Rhythmically he scraped the meadow, humming in time. He was like a woman rocking, suffering to bring her fruit into the light of day, moaning a gradual moan, until her ultimate scream.

Philippe opened his eyes, astonished, and came to his senses.

Hey!... What's the matter with me? I knew she had to leave before we did. I have her address in Paris, her phone number... besides, what difference does it make to me that she left? She's my mistress, not my love... I can live without her.

Sitting down, he plucked the rosaries of snails off the blades of grass the cows liked to munch. He tried his hand at laughter and grossness.

She's gone, fine. Maybe she's not alone. . . . She didn't pass the time by letting me in on all the details of her business, right? . . . Fine. Alone or not alone, she's gone. I'm losing . . . what? Tonight, tomorrow night. One night before I have to go. A night I wasn't even sure I wanted a little while ago. I was only thinking about Vinca. . . . Can't I make do without one night of fun?

But a sort of breath passed through his mind, swept away the locker room vocabulary, his false assurance, the inward sneering, leaving only a surface in his mind that was naked, chilled, a sharp awareness of what Camille Dalleray's departure meant.

Oh . . . she's gone . . . she's gone, out of reach, the woman who gave me . . . who gave me . . . how can I describe what she gave me? No name for it. She gave me. Ever since the day when I stopped being that little boy enchanted by Christmas, she's the only one who's given me. Given. She's the only one who could take it back, she took it back . . . .

His tan face began to blush, moisture stung his eyes. He unbuttoned his shirt and uncovered his chest, dug all ten fingers into his hair, acted like a boxer furiously leaping out of the ring, panted, and screamed out loud, in a hoarse, childish voice: "I wanted this night, this night!"

With his torso pressed against his fists, Philippe turned his face, his eyes, up toward the invisible Ker-Anna: already a heaped-up nimbus, occupying the southern skies, overpowered that deserted hilltop; and Philippe understood that an all-powerful malice had liquidated the very place where he had known Camille Dalleray.

Someone coughed a few feet below him on a path of melting sand where flat stones and logs, dozens of times wrestled into the shape of a rustic staircase, rolled dozens of times a year back down to the beach. Philippe saw a head turning gray, level with the meadow and slowly walking up toward him. Like all children, he was a virtuoso at disguise and he tidied up the disorder in him, the fury of a man betrayed, and waited, silently, calmly, for his father to reach him.

"Is that you, kid?"

"Yes, Papa."

"You're alone? Where's Vinca?"

"I don't know, Papa."

Almost without effort, Philippe kept on the mask, personable, lively, of a tan little boy. His father, facing him, looked the way his father did every day: a pleasant and human countenance, a bit fuzzy like cotton, with hazy edges, similar to all terrestrial beings not named Vinca, Philippe, or Camille Dalleray. Phil waited patiently for his father to regain his breath.

"You didn't take your rod, Papa?"

"Fishing? No, I went for a walk. Wouldn't you know it, that

Lequérec caught himself an octopus.... Look, see this walking stick? That's how long his tentacles were. Amazing. Just imagine how Lisette would've screamed! You be careful now when you go swimming."

"Don't be silly, Papa, it's not dangerous!"

Philippe realized he was being unfair. He had protested too vehemently, falsely—and too much like a little boy. His father's prominent gray eyes questioned his own; he could hardly bear that glance—frank, revealing, wiped clean of the insulating and protective mist that shields boys full of secrets who live with their parents.

"Does it bother you that we're leaving, kid?"

"Leaving?... But Papa..."

"Yes. If you're at all like me, it bothers you a little more each year. The region, the house. And then there's the Ferret family.... One day you'll know how unusual it is to have friends you spend the summer with year after year, and still on good terms.... Enjoy the rest of your vacation, kid. Two more days to have fun. Lots of children aren't as lucky as you...."

But as his father was speaking he was already on his way to becoming one of the Shadows again, though an ambiguous word, a glance, had yanked him apart from them. Philippe offered him his arm to climb up the crumbling slope, showing him that cool, pitying attention that a child condescends to give his father, whenever the father is a calm and mature man, and the son a tumultuous adolescent who has just invented love, the torments of the flesh, and pride in being alone in the midst of the world, suffering without asking for help.

When they reached the level of the flat, narrow lawn that the villa sat on, Philippe let go of his father's arm, wanted to go back down to the beach, to sit back down in his particular spot, which had been his for less than an hour now, in a precise corner of human solitude.

"Where are you going now, kid?"

"Down there, Papa...."

"Is it that important? Come inside a minute. I want to explain some things to you, some things about the villa. You know, we're coming to a decision, Ferret and me. We're buying it. Well, you already know that, you children have heard us talk about it long enough...."

Phil didn't answer, not daring either to lie or to admit the deafening buzzing that cut him off from family conversations.

"Come on, I'll explain the whole thing to you. I thought of it first—Ferret agreed—to expand the villa with two wings on the ground floor, so that their roofs would form balconies for the two master bedrooms upstairs.... You follow me?"

Phil nodded his head with a knowing air, and he honestly tried to listen. But no matter what he did, his mind lost its footing every time he heard a certain word, the word "corbeling," and in his thoughts he went back down the slope, to the spot where that maleficent little boy said to him. . . . "Corbeling . . . Corbeling . . . so I decided on corbeling." Meanwhile Phil nodded his head, and his glance, stamped with filial alertness, traveled from his father's face to the Swiss chalet roof of the villa, from the roof to Monsieur Audebert's hand that was sketching the new architectural plan in the air. "Corbeling . . . you get it? Ferret and I will do it. Or it might be you, along with the Ferret girl. . . . You never know who's going to live or die. . . ."

Ah, I'm listening again! Philippe exclaimed to himself, startled by his deliverance.

"Why are you laughing? It's nothing to laugh about. You kids never believe in death!"

"We do, too, Papa. . . ."

"Death . . . in the end, it's a familiar word, an understandable word . . . an everyday word. . . . Obviously it's very possible you and Vinca will get married later on. At least that's what your mother insists will happen. But then again, it's also very possible you won't marry her. What are you smiling about?"

"What you're saying, Papa. . . ."

What you're saying, and the simplicity of parents, mature people, those who, as they say, have lived, and their candor, and the disturbing purity of their thoughts. . . .

"Notice I'm not asking your opinion on this for now. You might say to me, 'I want to marry Vinca,' and it'd have just the same effect as if you'd said, 'I don't want to marry Vinca.'"

"Oh, really?"

"Yes. The time isn't ripe yet. You're very sweet, but..."

His prominent, gray eyes once again emerged out of the universal confusion and looked Philippe over.

"But you have to wait. That Ferret girl's dowry won't weigh in very heavy. Doesn't matter. You can easily get along without velvet, silk, and gold in the beginning...."

Velvet, silk, and gold... Oh, velvet, silk, and gold... red, black, white— red, black, white—and the ice cube, cut like a diamond, in the water glass.... My velvet, my luxury, my mistress and my master... how to get along without that excess....

"Work... difficult start... serious... time to think about... the times we live in...."

I hurt. Here, right around my stomach. And I'm terrified of that purple-blue rock, against the dark red background, the white and black I can see in me....

"Family life... Pampered... God!... Croissants first thing in the morning... son... what do you say? What do you say?"

His voice, his intermittent words were smothered by the sweet sound of encroaching water. Philippe could no longer perceive anything more than a weak shock to his shoulder and dry grass tingling against his cheek. Then the sound of several voices once again pierced, like so many sharp little islands, the sea's even and pleasant lowing, and Phil opened his eyes again. His head was resting on his mother's knees, and all the Shadows, in a circle, were leaning their innocuous faces over him. A handkerchief steeped in rubbing alcohol and lavender water brushed his nostrils, and he smiled at Vinca who placed herself, golden-colored, pinkish brown, crystal blue, between him and the Shadows.

"Poor baby!"

"Didn't I tell you he seemed ill?"

"The two of us were talking, there he was, right in front of me, and then Boom!"

"He's like all boys his age—incapable of watching what he eats. He stuffs his pockets full of fruit...."

"And what about their first cigarettes, don't forget those!"

"My darling boy! His eyes are full of tears..."

"That's a natural reaction..."

"Not only that, it lasted at most thirty seconds, the time it took to call you. Just like I said, there he was, we were talking, and then..."

Phil sat back up, lightheaded, his cheeks cold.

"Don't move yet! What are you doing!"

"Lean on me, son..."

But he held Vinca's hand, and smiled without expression.

"It's over now. Thanks, Mama. It's over now."

"Don't you want to get into bed?"

"No. I'd rather stay out in the fresh air."

"Look at Vinca's face! Your Phil isn't dead yet! Bring him over here. But stay as much as possible on the lawn!"

The Shadows went away, a slow swarm with friendly hands

reaching out and words of encouragement; a maternal look shined from it for the last time, and Philippe was left alone with Vinca, who was not smiling. With one gesture of his mouth, with one reassuring motion of his head, he pleaded with her to be happy, but she answered with a different gesture: "No," and continued to stare at Philippe, his pallor turning his sunburn slightly green, in his dark eyes the sunlight diluted to a reddish gleam, his mouth half opened over thick, little teeth. *You're so handsome... and I'm so sad!* said Vinca's blue eyes. But he read no pity in them, and she let him hold her rough hand, the hand of a fisherwoman, of a tennis player, as if she were holding out to him the head of a cane.

"Come with me," Philippe begged softly. "I can explain... it was nothing. But let's go someplace quiet."

She went with him, and somberly they chose for their secret chamber a rock flat as a table, sometimes dampened by the high tide, furnished by it with a rough-grained sand that quickly dried. Neither of them had ever believed that a secret could be confided to hangings of bright cretonne; to musically resonant, pitch pine partitions that carried at night from one room to the other the news that one of the villa's inhabitants was turning a light switch, coughing, or letting a key fall. Savages in their own way, these two children of Paris knew how to escape the indiscretions of human shelters, and sought privacy for their idylls and their dramas in the midst of an open meadow, at the edge of a rocky eyrie, or against the hollow flanks of a wave.

"It's four o'clock," said Philippe, consulting the sun. "You don't want me to get your afternoon snack before we sit down?"

"I'm not hungry," Vinca answered. "Do you want your snack?"

"No, thanks. That little shock I had took away my appetite. Sit at the back, I like it at the edge."

They spoke plainly, feeling they were close to serious words, or to a silence that would be almost as revealing.

The September sun glinted off Vinca's polished, brown legs that were folded up at the hem of her white dress. Below them, an inoffensive swell of the sea, licked and softened by a passing mist, danced softly, gradually took on the color of good weather. The gulls cawed, and a rosary of small craft dropped off one by one, as sail after sail left the shadow of Meinga and reached the high seas. A child's song, sharp and tremulous, passed by on the breeze; Philippe turned around, shuddered, and breathed a sort of irritated, plaintive sigh; at the top of the topmost cliff, in a bluish tunic, a red-haired little boy…

Vinca followed Philippe's glance.

"Uh huh," she said, "that's the boy."

Phil regained his composure.

"I guess you're talking about the boy from the fish store?"

Vinca shook her head No. "The boy," she corrected, "who spoke to you a little while ago."

"Who *what?*"

"The little boy who came to tell you that the lady left."

Suddenly Philippe hated the glare of daylight, the hard sand on his back, and the mild wind burning his cheek.

"Wha, what...what are you talking about, Vinca?"

She did not deign to answer but merely continued: "That boy was looking for you. He ran into me, and he told me first. Besides..." She ended with a fatalistic gesture. Phil breathed deeply, feeling a sort of well-being.

"Oh. Then you knew.... What did you know?"

"Things about you. I haven't known long. What I know I learned suddenly about...three or four days ago, but I had my suspicions."

She fell silent, and Philippe perceived, under her blue pupils, above his friend's fresh, childish cheek, the mother-of-pearl, the furrow of nocturnal tears and insomnia, that satin reflection, the color of moonlight, that one sees only under the eyes of women compelled to suffer in secret.

"Fine," said Philippe. "Then we can talk, unless you prefer not to.... I'll do whatever you want."

She repressed a little impulse that was at the corner of her mouth, but didn't cry.

"No, we can talk. I think it'd be better."

From the very first words of their conversation, they experienced a bitter and identical contentment in placing at a distance commonplace disputes and lies. Heroes, actors, and children are fated to feel comfortable on a higher plane. These children madly hoped that love could give rise to a sort of noble sadness.

"Listen, Vinca, when I met her the first time…"

"No, no," Vinca interrupted right away. "Not that. I don't want that from you. I know it already. Down there, at the end of the seaweed road. You think I forgot?"

"But nothing happened that day," Philippe protested, "either worth forgetting or remembering, since…"

"No, stop it! Stop it! You think I brought you here so you could tell me about *her?*"

He felt, from the unadorned harshness of Vinca's tone, that his own voice lacked any inflection of genuineness or contrition.

"You want to tell me your love story, is that it? Spare me. Last Wednesday when you came home I was awake, the lights were out…I saw you steal in like a thief…it was almost daylight. And your face.…So I made some inquiries, what did you think I'd do? Don't you realize everything that happens along this coast is common knowledge? Our parents are the only ones who don't know about it."

Philippe—shocked—frowned. That deep-seated feminine brutality, which jealousy had aroused in Vinca, hurt him. Once he had gotten to their airy refuge, he had felt capable of soft secrets, or of tears. He was inclined, in fact, to a lengthy confession. But he wouldn't accept that hypersensitive response, that sudden crudeness that sped right past the picturesque and flattering relay stations, and was heading toward... come to think of it, toward what?

I'm sure she wants to die, he said to himself. *She even wanted to die right here, one day.... She's going to want to die....*

"Vinca, you have to promise me..."

She listened to him without even glancing at him, and her whole body expressed, in that nimble motion, irony and independence.

"Vinca... you have to promise me that not on this rock, or anywhere else on earth... will you try to leave this life."

She dazzled him, directing the blue ray of her wide eyes right at him, with her blunt and unshaken look.

"What are you talking about? Leave... leave this life?"

He placed his hands on Vinca's shoulders, shaking a head heavy with experience: "I know you, honey. Right in this spot, you wanted, for no reason at all, to let yourself slide down there, just six weeks ago, and now..."

Amazement arched Vinca's eyebrows as she listened. With a twist of her shoulders she shook off Philippe's hands.

"Die? Now? Why should I?"

This last phrase made him blush, and Vinca considered his red face an answer.

"Because of her?" Vinca shouted. "Are you crazy?"

Annoyed, Phil ripped up tufts of thin grass and suddenly turned four or five years younger.

"You have to be crazy to figure out what a woman wants, assuming she even knows what she wants!"

"But I do know, Phil. I know perfectly well. And I also know what I don't want! You can relax, I'm not going to kill myself because of that woman! Six weeks ago I did let myself slide over there, down to the rocks, and I dragged you along with me. But that day I was going to die for your sake, and for mine, for mine...."

She shut her eyes, turned her head away. Her voice caressed the last few words, and strangely, she looked exactly like all women who let their head fall back and shut their eyes when flooded with happiness. For the first time, Philippe saw Vinca as a sister of the woman who, with her eyes closed and head flung back, seemed to separate herself from him at the very moment when he held her closest.

"Vinca! Hey, Vinca!"

She opened her eyes and sat up straight again.

"What is it?"

"Don't go away like that! You looked like you were swooning or something!"

"*I'm* not swooning, though I know how much you love it— the smelling salts, the cologne, all that trembling."

From time to time, childish ferocity slipped mercifully between them. They tapped its strength, steeped themselves once more in an anachronistic clarity, then threw themselves back into the madness of their elders.

"I'm going," said Philippe. "You're really hurting me."

Vinca laughed, a jerky, unpleasant laugh, like any woman who had been wounded.

"Oh, charming! Now you're the one who's been hurt, huh?"

"Sure I have."

She made a sound like the cry of a bird, irritated, piercing, unexpected. It made Philippe shudder.

"What's the matter with you?"

She had been leaning on her two open palms, almost on all fours, like an animal. He suddenly saw her as frantic, purple with rage. The two panels of her hair seemed to join in front of her tilted face, revealing only her red, dry mouth; her short nose, swollen by the anger she exhaled, and her two flame-blue eyes.

"Shut up, Phil! Shut your mouth! I hurt you! You complain, you talk about your pain! When you cheated on me, you lied to me! When you lied, when you left me for another woman! You have no shame, no sense, no pity! You brought me here just to tell me, me, me, what you did with that other woman! Go ahead, deny it. Go ahead!"

She screamed, comfortable in her feminine fury as a petrel in a squall. She sat back down as if falling, her hands groping and finding a fragment of rock that she hurled far into the water, with a strength that astonished Philippe.

"Shut up, Vinca..."

"No, I'm not going to shut up! First of all, we're all alone, and besides, I want to scream! I think I have something to scream about. You brought me here because you wanted to tell me, go over everything you did with her, for the pleasure of listening to yourself, to your words...of talking about her, of saying her name, huh? Wasn't it her name you wanted to say?"

She hit him in the face with a punch so unexpected and so like a boy's that he almost attacked her and fought back with all his might. The words she had just emphatically pronounced held him back and his deep-down, masculine decency recoiled in the face of what Vinca understood and had made him so bluntly understand.

She thinks, she believes that it would have given me pleasure to tell her the story.... Oh, and it's Vinca, Vinca who's thinking these things....

She fell silent a moment, coughed, red all the way down to her chest. Two little tears slipped from her eyes, but she wasn't ready yet for the sweetness and silence of tears.

Then I never realized what she was thinking? mused Philippe. *All her words are as surprising as that power I've often seen in her, when she's swimming, when she jumps, when she tosses stones....*

He didn't trust Vinca's movements and kept an eye on her. The radiant color of her complexion, of her eyes, the precision of her thin form, the fold of her white dress spread over her long legs all pushed away the almost sweet pain that had leveled him, motionless, on the grass....

He took advantage of the truce, wanting to look more composed than she did.

"I didn't hit you, Vinca. Your words deserved it more than your actions. But I didn't want to hit you. It would've been the first time I would've let myself go like that...."

"Naturally," she interrupted hoarsely. "You'll hit someone else before me. I won't be first at anything!"

The voraciousness of her jealousy reassured him, he almost broke into a smile, but Vinca's vindictive look made joking out of the question. They remained silent, saw the sun dipping behind Meinga and a pink stain, curved like a petal, danced at the crest of each wave.

Cowbells tolled at the top of the cliff. Where the ominous little boy had sung a little while ago, the horned head of a black goat appeared and bleated.

"Vinca darling..." Philippe sighed.

She looked at him indignantly.

"You dare to speak to me like that?"

He bowed his head.

"Vinca darling..." he sighed.

She bit her lips, gathered her forces against the assault of tears that she felt rising in her, tightening her throat, swelling her eyes, and didn't risk speaking. Philippe, leaning the nape of his neck against the rock embroidered with a close-cropped, violety foam, contemplated the sea and perhaps didn't see her. Because he was weary, because it was a beautiful evening, because of the hour and what its aroma and its melancholy demanded, he sighed: "Vinca darling…" as if he had been sighing, "I'm so happy!" or even: "I'm in such pain…." His newfound agony breathed out the most ancient words, the first words that came to his lips: just as the aging soldier, if he falls in battle, moans the name of his forgotten mother.

"Shut up. You're *evil!* Shut *up!* What have you done to me, what have you done?…"

She showed him her tears that left no furrows as they rolled down her velvet cheeks. The sun played on her overflowing eyes, expanding the blue of her irises. A lover, wounded by it all, magnanimous enough to forgive all, shone in all her splendor on the upper half of Vinca's face; a sad, slightly comical little girl grimaced prettily with her mouth and trembling chin.

Without giving up the support of his hard pillow, Philippe turned his black eyes on her, eyes softened by an appealing languor. Anger had squeezed out of this overheated young girl the aroma of a blonde woman, like the smell of the pink flower of the restharrow, or trampled green wheat, a lively and biting aroma that filled out the impression of strength that Vinca's gestures had made on Philippe. But she was crying, and stammering: "What have you *done* to me?…" She wanted to staunch her tears, and bit down on one of her hands where the semicircle of her young teeth stood out in purple.

"Savage," said Phil half to himself, with the tender attention that he would have given to a woman he didn't know.

"More than you know," she said, echoing his tone of voice.

"Then don't tell me!" shouted Philippe. "Every single word you speak sounds like a threat!"

"Before, you would have said 'a promise,' Phil!"

"Same thing!" he protested loudly.

"Why?"

"Because."

He chewed on a blade of glass, decided on a prudent silence, since he was incapable of expressing precisely in words his secret claim to mental freedom, to the right to tell diverting and polite lies, that his age and his first fling had awakened in him.

"Phil, I wonder how you're going to treat me later on."

She seemed disheartened, empty of arguments. But Phil knew how she could bounce back, magically recapturing all her power.

"Don't wonder," was his simple plea.

Later on, later on . . . yes, she's seized the future, too. . . . She's lucky to be able to think of the color of the future at a time like this! It's her need to move on that's talking. . . . She's a long way from wanting to die. . . .

He was too peevish to recognize the mission to endure—the lot of all species of females—and the august instinct to dig down into misfortune by exploiting it like a mine of precious minerals. With the help of the evening and his fatigue, he was overcome by this combative child, who fought with primitive weapons for the health of this couple. He tore his thoughts away from her, ran in mental pursuit of a car rolling on its horizontal cloud of dust, reached, like a beggar alongside the road, the window where a head dozed against it, turbaned in white veils. . . . He could see every detail of her again, her blackened eyelashes, the black beauty mark next to her lip, her palpitating and pinched nostrils, features he had only contemplated up close, oh! so close. . . . His mind straying, startled, he stood up, full of the fear of pain, and his surprise that, while he was talking to Vinca, his pain had ceased. . . .

"Vinca!"

"What's the matter?"

"I . . . I feel sick. . . ."

An irresistible arm lay hold of his own, made him fall down at the safest possible place on this scarped nest, since he was teetering at the edge. Dejected, he didn't put up a fight, and merely said:

"But maybe this is the simplest way out. . . ."

"Oh, my!"

She did not look for words beyond this trite exclamation. She laid the boy's weakened body against her, and pressed a brown head onto her breasts, rounded by a morsel of sweet, new flesh. Philippe gave in to his cowardly and recent habit of passivity, acquired in those luxurious arms; but if he was actually searching, with an almost unbearable bitterness, for that resinous perfume, that accessible chest, at least he effortlessly moaned the name of:

"Vinca darling . . . Vinca darling. . . ."

She gave in and cradled him, her arms gathered in and knees together, swaying with the rhythm of feminine creatures all over the world. She cursed him for being so unhappy and pampered. She wished he would go mad in his delirium and forget a certain woman's name. She spoke to him without speaking. *It's all right, it's all right... You'll come to know me... I'll show you...* but at the same time she brushed off of Philippe's forehead a black hair, like a thin crack in a block of marble. She savored the weight, the new contact with the body of a young man whom yesterday she still carried piggyback, laughing and running. When Philippe, half opening his eyes, sought out her glance with a look begging her to give back what he had lost, she slammed her hand down on the sand next to her and cried out from her very depths: "Why were you ever born!" like the heroine of an eternal drama.

Meanwhile her nimble eyes kept watch over the surroundings of the faraway villa; she gauged the sun's fall the way a sailor would: *It's after six o'clock.* She observed Lisette passing by between the beach and the house, fluttering in her dress like a white pigeon. *We'd better not stay here longer than fifteen minutes,* she thought, *or they'll come looking for us. I really have to wash my face...* then she brought back together body and soul, love, jealousy, her fury, reluctant to be calmed, havens of the mind as rugged and primordial as this nest in the rocks.

"Get up," she said softly.

Philippe complained, made himself heavier. She guessed that

he was now using his complaints, his inertia as a way of evading her criticisms and questions. Her arms, which had just seemed maternal, shook his bent neck, his warm torso—and this burden, once out of her embrace, became again the boy who lied, almost unrecognizable, a stranger, capable of betraying her, someone whom a woman's hands had polished and changed.

Tie him up, like the black goat, at the end of two meters of rope . . . Lock him up in a room, in my room . . . Live in another country where there are no women except me . . . Or I could be so beautiful, so beautiful that . . . Or he could be just sick enough for me to take care of him . . . The shadows of her thoughts drifted across her face.

"What are you going to do?" asked Philippe.

She thought, undeceived now, that his features later on would undoubtedly become those of a fairly humdrum, pleasant, dark-haired man; but that his seventeenth year still kept him a while longer on this side of virility. She was astonished that no stigmata, horrible and revealing, had marred that pleasant chin, that well-formed nose apt to show anger: *But his brown eyes, too soft, and their pale blue whites, oh! I can see now that a woman gazed in them. . . .* She shook her head:

"What am I going to do? Get ready for dinner. And so will you."

"That's it?"

Standing, she tugged on her dress below the elastic silk waistband and meticulously looked over Philippe, the house, the sea that was sleeping and refused, in its cooled grayness, to participate in the blaze of the sunset.

"That's it...unless *you* do something."

"What do you mean by 'something'?"

"Well...you could leave, go back and look for that woman...decide that she's the one you love...tell your parents."

She spoke in a hard and boyish way, pulling down unconsciously on her dress as if she wanted to flatten her breasts.

Her breasts are shaped like limpet shells...or like those little conical mountains in Japanese paintings....

He blushed because he had distinctly pronounced the word breasts to himself, and accused himself of disrespect.

"I won't do any of those ridiculous things, Vinca," he rushed to say. "But I would like to know how you'd react if I were capable of doing all of them, or at least half."

She opened her eyes wide, bluer for having cried, eyes in which he could read nothing.

"Me? I wouldn't change my way of life."

She lied and defied him, but beneath the lie of her glance he saw, he could feel, the tenacity, the constancy without respite or scruples that preserves a woman in love and ties her to the man she loves and to life, once she has discovered she has a rival.

"You sound more logical than you really are, Vinca."

"And you sound more stuck up than you really are. Didn't you think I wanted to die, just a little while ago? Die, because the Big Man had his little fling!"

She thrust her hand at him, open-palmed, the way children do when they squabble.

"A little fling..." Philippe repeated, wounded and flattered. "Why not? All the boys my age..."

"So I guess I'll just have to get used to the fact," Vinca interrupted, "that you're no better than 'all the boys' your age."

"Vinca, darling, I swear to you that a young girl shouldn't speak, shouldn't hear..."

He bowed his head, chewed his lips conceitedly, and added:

"Just take my word for it."

He offered his hand to Vinca so she could step over the long, schistous stonebeds lying at the entrance to their shelter, then the low bouquets of gorse that separated them from the customs path. Three hundred meters away, on the meadow by the sea, Lisette in white was turning like a white morning-glory, and her little brown arms gestured, telegraphed: "Come quickly! You're late!" Vinca lifted her arms, answered, but she turned back toward Philippe before beginning the trek down.

"The problem is, Phil, I can't believe you. Or our whole life up to now may only have been one of those insipid little stories in books we don't like. You say to me: 'a young man...a young girl' when you talk about us. You say, 'a little fling like all the boys my age...' But Phil, you're still in the wrong... See, I'm speaking perfectly calmly..."

He listened to her, a bit impatiently, and was perplexed when he sought at that very moment for the scattered embers and thorns of his great sorrow, and couldn't reassemble them. Vinca's extreme distress, visible under her exaggerated self-assurance, was about to disperse them again, and what's more, the evening wind was picking up with malevolent swiftness.

"Come on! What now?"

"You're still in the wrong, Phil, since you should've asked me..."

He was empty of desires, weary, dying to be alone, and yet full of apprehension at the threshold of a long night. She had expected an outburst from him, indignation, or rather an impure confusion: he measured her from head to toe, cutting his eyes at her, and said:

"Poor little Vinca! 'Ask you...'. Fine. To give what?"

He saw she was offended and speechless, the purple traces of her fiery blood that had risen to her cheeks now sank back down under the skin of her tan bosom. He threw an arm around her shoulders, and walked pressed against her down the path.

"Vinca darling, you see what silly things you're saying! Silly things from an inexperienced girl. Thank God for that!"

"Thank Him for something else, Phil. Don't you think I know as much as the first woman he created?"

She didn't move away, looked at him out of the corner of her eye, then looked ahead to the difficult path, then looked back at Philippe again, whose attention was caught by that angle of the eye that the pupil's motion made alternately periwinkle blue, and white as the nacreous throat of a shell.

"Tell me, Phil, don't you think I know, know as much as..."

"Shush, Vinca! You don't. You don't know anything."

He stopped their progress at a turn in the path. All the azure had fled from the sea, which had been cast into a solid gray metal, almost without folds, and the extinguished sun left a long, sad trace of red along the horizon, above which a pale zone reigned, green, brighter than the dawn, where the moist star that rose first would steep. With one arm Philippe pressed Vinca's shoulders. He stretched the other toward the sea.

"Shush, Vinca! You don't know anything. It's...too much of a secret... Too grown up."

"I'm grown up."

"No, you don't understand what I'm trying to tell you."

"Yes, I do, I understand perfectly well. You act like the Jalons' little boy, the one who's a choirboy on Sundays. To sound important he says, 'Latin! Oh, you know how incredibly hard Latin is!' but he doesn't even know Latin."

Suddenly she laughed, her head tilted back, and Philippe was not at all pleased that she glided, in just a few seconds and so naturally, from tragedy to laughter, from consternation to irony.

Perhaps because night was falling, he began to miss that calm shot through with voluptuous fire, a silence where the blood, surging in his ears, imitated the rushing of rain. He yearned for fear, to be almost dumbfounded by its dangerous sway, that had bent his back at a threshold other adolescents had crossed staggering and blaspheming.

"Shut up now, Vinca. Don't act bad and vulgar. When you know..."

"But all I want is to know!"

Her speech sounded false, and she laughed the laugh of a clumsy actor to hide the fact that inside her everything was trembling, and that she was just as sad as all children who have been scorned and who seek, at serious risk to themselves, a chance to suffer a bit more, and even a bit more than that, and still more, until they get their reward....

"I'm begging you, Vinca! You're hurting me... That doesn't sound like you at all, that way of talking!"

He dropped the arm he had put around Vinca's shoulder, and walked faster down toward the villa. She went with him, and when the path narrowed she jumped over the tufts of grass already impregnated with dew; as she walked she composed her face for the consumption of the Shadows, repeating half-out-loud for Philippe:

"Not at all like me? Not at all like me? Well, there's something you don't know about me, Phil—Mr. Know-It-All."

The two of them, sitting at the dinner table, behaved in a manner worthy of each other and their secrets. Philippe laughed about his "fainting spell," demanded they take care of him, drew attention to himself because he was afraid that they would notice the glittering eyes, surrounded by a bruised pink, that Vinca sheltered under her silky thatch, trimmed to a thick fringe above the eyebrows. Vinca, on the other hand, was playing the child; she demanded champagne with the soup course: "It's to revive Phil, Mama!" and downed her wide glass of Pommery in one breath.

"Vinca!" scolded a Shadow.

"Leave her alone," said another, more indulgent Shadow. "What harm can it do her?"

Near the end of dinner, Vinca saw Philippe's glance searching the nocturnal sea for the invisible form of Meinga, the white road that had melted into the night, the petrified juniper trees covered by the dust of the road....

"Lisette," she shouted, "pinch Phil, he's falling asleep!"

"Hey! She pinched me so hard she drew blood!" Philippe moaned. "You little brat! You almost made me cry!"

"It's true, it's true!" said Vinca in a shrill voice. "She made you cry!"

She laughed while he rubbed his arm against his white flannel jacket; but he could see in Vinca's cheeks, in her eyes, the flame of the sparkling wine and a sort of prudent madness he found not at all reassuring.

A bit later on a foghorn bellowed far in the distance over the black swells, and one of the Shadows ceased stirring the stipple-bellied dominoes on the card table.

"Fog over the water..."

"The Granville Light looked like it was sweeping through cotton just now," said another Shadow.

But the foghorn's sirenlike voice had just evoked the lowing horn of an automobile fleeing along the coast road, and Philippe jumped to his feet.

"He's having a relapse!" kidded Vinca.

Good at hiding, she turned her back on the Shadows and her gaze followed Philippe like a lament.

"I am not," said Philippe. "But I am exhausted, and I'd like to be excused to go to bed. G'night, Mama, g'night, Papa. G'night, Madame Ferret. G'night..."

"That's all right, m'boy, you don't have to recite the whole litany tonight."

"Should I bring you up a cup of chamomile, just lightly brewed?"

"Don't forget to open your window really wide!"

"Vinca, did you bring Phil your smelling salts?"

The friendly voices of the Shadows followed him to his door, like a protective garland, a bit wilted, with the sweet, faded perfume of dried herbs. He exchanged with Vinca their everyday kiss, which always fell near the offered cheek and slid toward the ear, on the neck, or on the downy corner of the mouth. Then his door closed again, the propitious garland fell neatly apart, and he was alone.

His room, yawning at the moonless night, greeted him coldly. Standing under the bulb swathed in yellow muslin, he breathed in, hostile and delicate, the smell that Vinca called "the boy smell"—old copies of classic books, a leather valise ready for their departure the day after tomorrow, rubber soles like asphalt, fine soap, and scented rubbing alcohol.

He was not particularly in pain. But he experienced a sensation of exile and total exhaustion that demanded just one remedy: oblivion. He quickly got into bed, turned his lamp off, and instinctively looked for the spot, against the wall, where his boyish sorrows, his growing pains had found the protective night, the shelter of the well tucked-in sheet, the flowered wallpaper where his dreams unfurled, borne up by the full moon, the high tide, or the storms of July. He fell asleep right away, only to be attacked by the most intolerable and typical details of the dreamworld. Here Camille Dalleray appeared with Vinca's features, over there Vinca, tyrannical, ruled over him with a coolness that suggested impurity and prestidigitation. But in his dream neither Camille Dalleray nor Vinca cared to recall that Philippe was just a tender shoot of a boy, eager just to lay his head on someone's shoulder, a little boy just ten years old....

He woke up, saw that his watch said a quarter to twelve and

that this botched night would smolder feverishly in the midst of a sleeping house; he put on his sandals, knotted his bathrobe around his waist, and went downstairs.

The moon in its first quarter was shaving the cliff. Curved and reddish, it lent no brightness to the landscape, and the whirling light of the Granville Light seemed, with each red beam, with each green beam, to extinguish it. But because of the moon the night did not submerge the masses of greenery, and between its exposed beams the villa's rough, white plaster glowed faintly phosphorescent. Philippe left the glass door open, and entered that sweet night as if it were a safe and sad haven. He sat down on the very lawn that was impervious to moisture, trampled and crammed with sixteen summers of vacation, where Lisette's shovel had sometimes exhumed, antique and oxidized, a fragment of a toy that had been interred for ten, twelve, fifteen years.

He felt sorry, wise, distant from everyone. *Maybe this is what it's like to become a man,* he mused. His unconscious need to consecrate his sadness and wisdom tormented him in vain, as it tormented all the honest young atheists whose secular education does not admit God as a spectator.

"Is that you, Phil?"

The voice drifted down to him like a leaf on the wind. He stood up, walked silently to the window with the wooden balcony.

"Yes," he whispered. "You're not asleep?"

"Well, obviously not. I'm coming downstairs."

She joined him but he didn't hear her approach. All he could see coming toward him was a bright face, hovering above a silhouette mingled with the hue of the night.

"You'll be cold."

"No, I put on my blue kimono. Anyway, it's mild. Let's not stay here."

"Why couldn't you sleep?"

"I'm not tired. I'm thinking. Let's not stay here. We'll wake somebody."

"I don't want you going down to the beach at this hour. You'll catch cold."

"Catching cold isn't my style. But I don't have any desire to go to the beach. Actually, why don't we just walk up a ways."

Her voice was elusive but Philippe didn't miss a single word. The lack of an edge to it gave him infinite pleasure. It wasn't Vinca's voice any more, or the voice of any woman. A slight presence, almost invisible, with a familiar tone of voice, a slight presence, without bitterness or intentions beyond this walk, beyond this tranquil vigil....

He stumbled against something and Vinca pulled him back by his hand.

"Those are the geraniums pots, can't you see them?"

"No."

"Me neither. But I see them the way blind people do, I know

they're there.... Pay attention, I think there's a spade on the ground right next to them."

"How do you know?"

"I just have a notion there's one there. And it would make a racket like a coal shovel... Boom!... What did I tell you?"

This mischievous whispering charmed Philippe. He could have cried with relief and pleasure, seeing Vinca so sweet, so similar in the shadows to the Vinca of old, who whispered like that when she was twelve years old, bent over the wet sand where the full moon danced over fish bellies, during their midnight fishing expeditions.

"You remember, Vinca, the night we went fishing at midnight, you caught the fattest flounder..."

"And you caught bronchitis! They sure made it clear we were never to commit that sin again.... Listen, did you close the glass door?"

"No."

"See, the wind is picking up and the door is banging. What would you do if you didn't have me to think of these things?"

She disappeared, returned sylphlike and so light on her feet that Phil guessed when she had come back by the perfume the wind carried ahead of her.

"What's that scent on you, Vinca? You really smell like perfume!"

"Shhh, quiet. I was hot, so I rubbed on a little cologne before I came downstairs."

He didn't respond, but his newly revived attention testified to how much, in fact, Vinca thought of everything.

"Go ahead, Phil. I'm holding the door. Don't walk on the lettuce."

In the incense that rose from the tilled earth of the vegetable garden, one could forget the nearness of the sea. A low, dense barrier of thyme grated against Phil's bare legs, and as he passed, his face brushed against the snapdragons' velvet muzzles.

"You realize, Vinca, that from the vegetable garden you can't hear the noise in the house, because of that cluster of trees."

"There isn't any noise in the house, Phil. And we're not doing anything wrong."

She had just picked up a little pear that had fallen from a tree. It was precociously ripe and musky from the worm inside it.

He heard her bite into the fruit, then toss it away.

"What are you doing? Eating?"

"It's one of the yellow pears. But it wasn't good enough for me to give you."

Her high spirits did not totally dissolve Philippe's vague suspicions. He thought Vinca a bit too sweet, lighthearted, and serene, like a spirit, and suddenly her peculiar joviality made her seem like someone escaped from the tomb, her kindness had the manic ring of the laughter of nuns. *I want to see her face,* he said to himself. And he shuddered to imagine that her voice without an edge, her playful, girlish words could come out of a grimacing mask, sparkling with the fury and the beautiful colors that had confronted his own mask in the nest in the rocks.

"Listen, Vinca, let's go back."

"If you want. One minute more. Give me one minute. I feel good. Do you? We feel good. It's so easy to live at night! But not in bedrooms. Oh, I've hated my room for several days now. Here, I'm not afraid of anything.... A glowworm! This late in the season! No, I shouldn't pick it up.... Why are you trembling, silly? Come on, that's just a cat going by. Cats hunt for field mice at night."

He could make out a little laugh, and Vinca's arm squeezed his waist. He listened closely to every sigh, every crackling, seduced, despite his worries, by the nuances in this whispering that didn't let up. Far from being apprehensive about the shadows, Vinca guided herself through them as if they were a friendly and familiar terrain, explained them to Philippe, played the hostess of midnight with him and walked him through it as if he were a blind guest.

"Vinca, darling, let's go back...."

She let fly a tiny "Oh!" like a toad.

"You called me 'Vinca darling'! Oh, why can't it always be night! Right at this moment you're not the same person who deceived me, I'm not the same person who felt so much pain.... Phil, let's not go back just yet, let me be a little happy, a little bit in love, sure of you the way I was in my dreams, Phil.... Phil, you don't know me."

"Maybe not, Vinca my darling..."

They tripped over a sort of hard hay that snapped.

"It's the threshed buckwheat," said Vinca. "They threshed it with the flails today."

"How do you know?"

"Didn't you hear them beating it with those two flails while we were arguing? I heard it. Sit down, Phil."

I can't believe she heard that... she was frantic, she slapped me in the face, she let out an unbroken stream of words—but she heard the two flails threshing.

Involuntarily he compared the vigilance of all her feminine senses to his memory of another feminine skill....

"Don't go away, Phil! I haven't been bad, I haven't cried or accused you of anything...."

Vinca's round head, her silken and even hair rolled onto Philippe's shoulder and the warmth of her cheek warmed his cheek.

"Kiss me, Phil, please, please..."

He kissed her, mixing with his own pleasure the disinclination of extreme youth that aims only to gratify its own desire, and the all-too-precise memory of another kiss, that was ripped away from him. But he learned with his lips the shape of Vinca's, the taste she retained of the fruit she had incised earlier, the rush of that mouth to open, to disclose and squander its secret—and he staggered in the shadows. *I hope,* he thought, *that we're lost. May we be lost quickly then, since it has to be, since she no longer wants it any other way.... My God, Vinca's mouth is so inevitable and deep, so knowing after the first shock.... Oh, may we be lost quickly, quickly...*

But possessing another is a laborious miracle. An arm, that he couldn't succeed in unknotting, was madly binding the nape of Philippe's neck. He shook his head to free it, and Vinca, thinking that Philippe wanted to break off their kiss, squeezed harder. Finally he grabbed the stiff fist next to his ear and threw Vinca down onto the bed of buckwheat. She moaned for a moment and didn't move, but when he leaned over her, ashamed, she took him back and spread him out against her. They forged a charming and almost fraternal truce, where each of them showed a touch of pity and kindness, the discretion of steadfast lovers. Philippe held in his arm an invisible Vinca, flung back, but his free hand smoothed a skin whose softness and marks he was not unaware of, marks etched by the point of a thorn and the horn of a rock. She tried to laugh for a second, softly pleading:

"Leave my beautiful scratch alone.... It makes the shelled buckwheat feel so soft...."

But he heard her breath trembling through her voice, and he trembled, too. He returned endlessly to what he knew the least about Vinca, her mouth. He decided, while they were catching their breath, to jump up and run back to the house. But as he moved away from Vinca he was seized by a pang of physical deprivation, by a horror of chilled air and empty arms, and he came back to her, with an enthusiasm that she mirrored and that tangled their knees. He found the strength then to name her "Vinca darling" in a humble tone that begged her simultaneously to encourage and forget his advances. She understood, and out of exasperation just kept silent, perhaps too silent, and she hurried so much that she bruised herself. He heard her short, mutinous complaint, felt her involuntarily lash out, but the body he was transgressing against did not slip away, and rejected any clemency.

He slept little and deeply and woke up feeling the whole house was empty. But downstairs, he saw the watchman and his taciturn dog, also his own fishing tackle, and he heard, upstairs, his father's daily cough. He hid between the spindle-tree hedge and the lawn wall and watched Vinca's window. A lively breeze chased away the clouds, melted by its breath. Turning the other way, Phil saw the sails of Cancale leaning against a short and hard billow of a wave. All the windows of the house were still sleeping.

Is she sleeping, though? They always say girls cry afterward. Vinca might be crying at this very moment. This is the time she should be resting against my arm, the way we used to on the sand. Then I'd say to her, "It isn't true. Nothing happened! You're still the Vinca you've always been. You didn't give me that pleasure, which wasn't such a great pleasure. Nothing is true, not even that sigh and that song, suddenly left hanging, that all at once made you leaden and long as if you'd died in my arms. Nothing is true. If tonight, I disappeared at the top

of the white road toward Ker-Anna, and if I came back alone before tomorrow's
sunrise, I'd hide so well you wouldn't ever know. . . . Let's go for a walk along
the shore, and we'll bring Lisette."

He couldn't imagine that a pleasure badly given, badly
received, is a perfectible work. The nobility of youth led him only
to salvage what he couldn't let die: fifteen years of enchantment,
a special tenderness, their fifteen years as twins, pure and in love.

I'll say to her: "Obviously our love, the love of Phil-and-Vinca, leads
somewhere other than there, there, that bed of threshed buckwheat, bristling with
straw. It leads somewhere other than the bed in your room or mine. Obviously.
Of course. Believe me! Since a woman I don't even know gave me a joy so
solemn it still makes me throb even though I'm far away from her, like the heart
of an eel, torn out of the eel while it was still beating, think of what our love
can do for us. Obviously. Of course . . . but if I fooled myself, you can't ever
know that I fooled myself. . . ."

I'll say to her: "It was a premature dream, a delirium, a torture that made
you bite your hand, my poor friend, you assisted bravely while I performed my
cruel duty. For you it was a dream, maybe horrible; for me, a worse humiliation,
a voluptuousness less enjoyable than the surprises of my solitude. But nothing is
lost if you forget all that, and if I erase that memory, mercifully hidden by the
darkness . . . No, I didn't squeeze your supple flanks between my knees—let me
ride piggyback, grabbing your shoulders, and let's go run along the beach. . . ."

When he heard the curtains sliding on their rod, he
summoned all his courage and managed not to look away.

Vinca appeared between the shutters that she pushed out

against the wall. She squinched her eyes closed a few times, and looked out with a passive firmness. Then she plunged her hands into her thick hair, and plucked from its disorder a dry twig. A smile and a blush broke out at the same time on her tilted face, framed by her jumbled hair. No doubt she was searching for Philippe. Now completely awake, she went back into the room and picked up a glazed clay pitcher and carefully watered a crimson fuchsia that adorned the wooden balcony. She consulted the fresh blue sky, promising good weather, and began to sing the song she sang every day. Between the spindle trees, Philippe watched like a criminal waiting to attack.

She's singing... I can't believe my eyes and ears, she's singing. And she just watered the fuchsia.

Not for one second did he consider that such an apparition, perfectly in keeping with the vow he had just made, should bring him joy. He couldn't stop thinking of how deceived she was, and too much of a novice to analyze this, he persisted in making comparisons:

One night, I collapsed in front of this window because a revelation had just fallen on me, thundering between my childhood and my life today. And all she does is sing....

The blue of Vinca's eyes rivaled the morning sea. She combed her hair and resumed her little song, this time humming. Her vague smile reappeared.

She's singing. She'll look beautiful at breakfast. She'll shout: "Lisette, pinch

*him till he bleeds!" Nothing particularly good, nothing particularly bad . . . She's
unscathed. . . .*

He saw that Vinca, leaning over, was pressing her chest
against the wooden balcony to look over at Philippe's room.

*If I appeared in the window next to hers, jumped over the balustrade to join
her, then she'd throw her arms around my neck.*

*You—the one I called "my master"—why did you sometimes seem more
filled with wonder than that fresh young girl, who looks so natural? You left
without telling me everything. Even if you were fond of me only out of a
benefactor's pride, you would pity me today, for the first time. . . .*

From the open window came a faint and happy humming,
but it didn't touch him. Nor did it occur to him that in a few
weeks the child who was singing might cry, might feel scared or
damned standing at the same window. He hid his face in the
crook of his elbow and contemplated his own smallness, his fall,
his merely benign impact. *Neither hero nor hangman . . . A little sadness,
a little pleasure . . . That's all I'll give her . . . that's all. . . .*

· THE AUTHOR ·

Colette, whose real name was Sidonie-Gabrielle Colette, was born in the village of Saint-Sauveur-en-Puisaye in Burgundy, France, in 1873 and died in Paris in 1954. Her many books include *Gigi* (1944), *The Vagabond* (1912), *Cheri* (1929), and *The Last of Cheri* (1932). She is considered one of the great novelists of the twentieth century. Among her many awards, Colette was made a member of the Belgian Royal Academy in the 1930s and was also the first woman to be admitted to the prestigious Goncourt Academy. In 1953 she became a grand officer of the Legion of Honour. A legendary figure who lived a colorful and bohemian life, she left behind writings rich with the joys and pains of love and sexual knowledge.

· THE TRANSLATOR ·

Zack Rogow translates French literature, and was a co-winner of the PEN/Book-of-the-Month Club Translation Award for *Earthlight*, by André Breton, as well as winner of a Bay Area Book Reviewers Award (BABRA) for his translation of George Sand's novel, *Horace*. His translations have appeared in a variety of magazines, including *The American Poetry Review, The Paris Review, Antaeus,* and *Two Lines.* He serves on the board of directors of the Center for Art in Translation. He is the editor of a new anthology of U.S. poetry, *The Face of Poetry,* to be published by University of California Press in 2005. His essays and reviews have been published in *The New York Times Book Review, AWP Writer's Chronicle, The San Francisco Chronicle, Poets & Writers Magazine,* and other publications. At the University of California, Berkeley, he coordinates the Lunch Poems Reading Series. He teaches in the M.F.A. in Writing Program at the California College of the Arts, and lives in San Francisco.